I0628451

It's Just a Spleen and a High School Ring

By

Joyce Foy

Copyright © 2017 Joyce Foy

All Rights Reserved. No part of this publication may be reproduced, stored in a retrieval system or transmitted in any form or by any means...electronic, mechanical, photocopy, recording of any other, except for the brief quotations in printed reviews without prior permission of the publisher.

Library of Congress: 1-4474572631
ISBN: 978-0-9968437-9-9

Requests for Information should be addressed to:
www.AVegasPublisher.com
avegaspublisher@yahoocom

First Edition 2003
Second Edition 2017
Trade Paperback

Acknowledgements

To the citizens of Zavalla, Texas, without whom this book would have no life. Many characters and situations in this book, while based in fact from a real case I investigated, for all practical purposes have been fictionalized. Any resemblance to persons living or dead other than those listed below are purely coincidental.

Cotton Gascamp, Zavalla's former sheriff, who issued me more than one traffic ticket for speeding, but grew to be a good friend and respect the investigator in me.

Red Opal for inviting me into her home and sharing Zavalla's history and for all the other Opals I never had a chance to meet.

John Blackburn, my loving cousin, whose resemblance to Johnnie Blake is more than coincidental. He's a retired PI from San Francisco.

Gina Gribow a lovely young lady who has become a talented and beautiful attorney in the Coachella Valley near Palm Springs.

The Texas Rangers for their honesty and hard work

maintaining peace and tranquility in an otherwise hostile environment.

To a beautiful and floppy-eared Maggie May and her Riverside County Canine Officer, Coby Webb. For Maggie's tenacity in finding missing children and bringing bad guys to justice, I thank you. Have a cookie on me!

Chapter One

*Three words changed a mother's life forever, "My child's missing."
Add three more, "Please help me." That's how Camellia (Mel)
Walker's day began.*

"Rosa, you know I don't do investigations that involve missing
children. It's just too emotional for me," Mel Walker said.

"How many favors have I asked you for in all the years my
family and I have worked for you?" Rosa stood in the middle
of the room, one hand on a hip, a wooden spoon in the other.

Camellia "Mel" Walker graduated from the University of
California at Irvine with a Criminal Justice degree. Her inquis-
itive spirit, fearless soul, and having a hard-boiled cop for a
father, kept her focused on her future, to be an investigator
with her own business.

"None as far as I remember, Rosa, but my area of expertise
doesn't include finding children."

"All the time you say, 'Cases are no different. You follow
your instincts and you get your man.' That's all I'm asking you
to do."

"When that hit and run driver killed my Willie," Mel picked up a small picture frame from the corner of her desk, "my life changed forever." She wiped the glass with her shirttail, her eyes glistened. Willie wore baseball blue pajamas. In his arms, he clutched his favorite bear that had one ear missing. His blonde hair and blue eyes smiled at her from the recesses of her memory and the love she carried for him even today, several years later.

Rosa's voice brought Mel back to the present, "Will you, at least, talk with the mother? That's all I'm asking you to do right now, listen to her story."

"I have so many new cases now. I don't know where to begin. The District Attorney wants one finished in the next twenty-four hours. I'm really busy." Mel tore a piece of note paper from a pad and said, "Why don't I give you a name of another investigator friend of mine?"

"Why don't we get on the road to the mother's house? I know you're going to do this. I don't know why you're being so obstinate."

Mel handed the paper to Rosa and said, "With the balls I have in the air right now, many with major deadlines, why would I drop everything and work on this case for you?"

"Because Angel Boudreaux was Willie's schoolmate, that's why."

Chapter Two

"So, where are we going?" Mel asked.

"Go up Pacific Coast Highway toward Long Beach, and I'll tell you where to turn. You remember the yard sale we worked at Su Casa?" Rosa asked.

"The battered women's shelter? Sure."

"That's where Angel and her mother Dee live. When you see Angel's picture, you may remember her from some of the school programs. Get into the right lane at the next light."

"I'm only going over here to appease you. I'll listen to her story and give her a referral."

"Right." Rosa looked out the side window and smiled.

As they turned the corner into the urban community, Rosa directed Mel toward an interior street. The small frame houses, circa early 1950s, boasted aged asphalt driveways and rough brown shingle roofs. Mel stopped at a stop sign and yielded to an oncoming vehicle, then looked in her rearview mirror and spotted a familiar car, a pumpkin-colored Mustang.

"What's Johnnie doing here?" Mel asked.

"Two investigators are better than one?" Rosa suggested.

Mel pulled her vintage Mercedes to the curb in front of a house. A heavily barred front door and windows spoke volumes of crime in the area. Johnnie Blake stopped his Mustang behind Mel's car. He'd been working for Mel's company, Walker Investigations, conducting criminal and civil investigations for several years.

"Hi," Johnnie said, as he approached the two.

"Hi, yourself. Do I feel a set-up here?" Mel asked.

"Rosa thought we might double-team on this one. That is if you need me."

"Why don't you do the investigation yourself?"

"Because I think this case needs a woman's touch."

"What a chauvinist remark. Besides Johnnie, you're the most sensitive man I know."

"I may be gay and proud honey, but don't ask me to handle the tears. I don't do tears."

The threesome walked to the front door, rang the bell, and waited. Someone inside the house slid a small window cut-out in the door to one side and asked, "Can I help you?"

Rosa answered. "We're here to see Dee. We have an appointment. It's about Angel."

The thin, quiet woman directed Mel, Rosa, and Johnnie to a small sitting area off the living room. A sagging sofa with a faded floral pattern faced a small brick fireplace. Two straight-back wooden chairs lined one side of the sofa, and two aluminum chairs covered in plastic faced those. Despite the oppressive outside heat, the heavily lined drapes that covered the front window made the room appear smaller and darker. The walls were free of pictures or decorations. The house smelled of disinfectant: fresh and sanitary.

Mel chose to sit on one edge of the sofa. Johnnie bumped

against a floor lamp causing the fringe on the shade to shake.

Rosa had circled the room once when a cherub-face woman-child entered the room. Rosa embraced her, and then led the introductions.

"Mel, Johnnie, this is our new friend, Dee Boudreaux."

"Hello Dee," Mel said, as she extended her hand.

Dee wore an oversized well-worn gingham dress that hung from her slumped shoulders. Even the dress pockets sagged. Thread from the frayed hem clung to Dee's bare legs. The fragile handshake and tenuous quality in Dee's voice whispered screams of a down-trodden life. Although partially covered by makeup, the discolored bruise covering the left side of her face and into her hairline shouted secrets – a mother in pain.

She thrust a crumpled picture into Mel's hands. "This is my Angel. My perfect child, my only daughter. She's missing. Please help me find her."

The floodgates opened, and Dee burst into tears.

Chapter Three

Dee handed an open shoe box to Mel and Johnnie, who pored over several documents. They withdrew a copy of Angel's birth certificate, photos of Dee with her husband Henry Lee Boudreaux during happier days of their marriage, and a trust deed for some property in Texas. But it was the class photo of Angel poking Willie and smiling conspiratorially that cast the swing vote.

"Dee, how long have you been married?" Mel asked.

"Almost ten years. Most of that was hell. He beat me for cold toast, for Friday nights, and for no reason at all."

Mel noticed a freshly healed scar on Dee's forearm. "How'd this happen?"

"Henry Lee came home drunk one Friday night, and I asked him if he had the money to pay the rent. He grabbed the knife I was using to cut the chicken with and stabbed me."

"How long have you been at the shelter?" Johnnie asked.

"This time only a week." Dee pointed to her face. "This time it was my fault. He ran out of beer."

Johnnie asked, "Did you drink it?"

"No, I don't drink," she replied. Then added, "Why do you ask?"

"Why is it your fault? If his legs aren't broke, he can get off his duff, go to the store, and buy his own beer."

"Oh, I never thought of that. Anyway, all told, Angel and I have been in and out of shelters almost six years. It took me a long time to get the courage to take Angel and leave Henry. I do love him, but I can't have him hurting Angel, and he was starting to spank and slap her for little things. Sometimes he beat her for no reason, too. I was afraid the abuse would, as the counselors say, 'escalate.' I know this is all my fault. I brought all this on me and Angel."

"Don't blame yourself," Rosa said.

"Rosa's right. You must not take the responsibility for someone else's actions. You did the right thing for you and Angel. Your safety comes first." Johnnie said.

"Thank you so much for understanding."

"Anyway, tell us what happened the last time you saw her?" Mel asked.

"Two days ago, I got her ready that morning, and we had breakfast. She carried her little lunch box and books, and I walked her to school."

"What was she wearing?"

"Blue jeans with yellow sunflowers sewn on one hip and on one knee. I sewed them on to cover some worn spots. We don't have any new clothes to speak of. And a tee shirt. It was kind of a faded yellow. Oh, and pink tennies."

"Why didn't you pick her up after school?" Mel asked.

"I had a job interview that afternoon. So, I asked another mother here at the shelter to pick Angel up when her own daughter, who's only two years older, got out of school."

"Did Angel know that your friend would be there?" Mel asked.

"Yes, we discussed it that morning. I made this very clear."

"What happened after school?" Johnnie asked.

"My friend and her daughter stood outside Angel's exit and waited. When Angel didn't come out in twenty minutes or so, they went to her classroom. But she wasn't there either." Dee took a deep breath, her voice cracked.

"Did you call the police?" Johnnie asked.

"Yes, of course. My friend knew where I'd be interviewing and called me. I rushed to the school. The principal called Angel's teacher at home. The police even questioned several of her classmates." Dee cried. "She had a happy day at school, colored some art paper, played at recess, then just disappeared."

"Why do you think Henry Lee took her?" Mel asked.

"He had threatened to, many times. We've been in custody court a half dozen times. He doesn't want her — if you know what I mean. He just doesn't want me to have her. If he got custody, he'd simply drop her off with his family. He rarely has a sober day. His best friend is Jack."

"What's Jack's last name?" Johnnie asked.

"You know, Jack Daniels." She sighed, "Anyway, he can barely clothe and feed himself. She's baggage to him, and Henry Lee travels light."

"Did you try to reach him?" Mel asked.

"I contacted his family in Texas and in Louisiana, those with phones anyway. Of course they denied having her, seeing him, or knowing anything about it."

"Maybe he didn't take her. We need to consider another option here."

"Johnnie's right." Mel said. "We're assuming here. What if

she was abducted? I mean taken by a stranger and Henry Lee had nothing to do with this?"

"I know Henry Lee took her. She would never have gotten into a car with a stranger. That's one thing we've talked about since she was small. She would never..." Dee twisted a tissue between her soap-wrinkled fingers.

"Much as I hate to say this Dee, she could have been taken against her will." Johnnie said.

"The police told me that. But she would have fought, tried to bite him, and hollered out 'FIRE' just like we practiced. Someone would have seen it. Would have heard her cry for help. She wouldn't have left the school grounds without an escort. There were hundreds of people milling around the door, parked in the street, visiting. Someone would have noticed."

"So, what are the police doing?" Mel asked. "This is a case they'll probably refer to the FBI, especially if you feel Henry Lee's taken her out of state."

"They said an agent would be investigating and will call me."

Mel patted Dee's arm. "I know several guys in the Long Beach Police Department, and I know the FBI. They're the best team for this job. Their resources cannot be beaten."

Dee clutched Mel's hand. "You're the one I want. I want a mother who cares. One who understands the loss of a child." She began to cry.

So did Mel and Rosa.

Johnnie stood. "Oh yeah. That'll work."

Chapter Four

By early the next morning everyone's roles had been defined. Dee would stay in touch with Johnnie. Johnnie took over all Mel's assignments as well as his own. Despite Mel's fear of flying, she caught a plane for Texas. Rosa's duties included feeding and calming Dee and Johnnie and fretting over Mel's safety.

During the two-hour plane ride, Mel called Xavier Ramirez, a detective with the Harbour Pointe Police Department. Everyone called him X-Ray. Mel called him a brother she always wanted.

"You're where, Mel?"

"On a plane to Houston."

"Because?"

"I'm on a case."

"And you'll see Lucas, of course."

"Jesus, in all this rush I forgot about him being there."

"What kind of case?"

"The child abduction kind."

"You don't do domestic cases. Remember? Those make

you the bullets between a mother and a father, and you're the one who'll get hurt."

"I know. It's a long story. Her name is Angel, no middle name, Boudreaux. She's eight-years-old and was taken three days ago from her Long Beach school. Mother, Dee, short for Deidra, Boudreaux, lives in a shelter at Su Casa and believes the father, Henry Lee Boudreaux, took the child. Could you please call the Long Beach PD and the FBI and see what you can get for me, then email me at the office? Johnnie will take it from there."

"That's a good idea. Let the police and the FBI handle this Mel."

"It isn't that easy."

Her next call was to Lucas' home in Houston. The answering machine picked up. "Hi, Lucas here. Only I'm not. Please leave a message, and I'll return your call. Thanks."

"Hi, honey. It's Mel. Guess what? I'm on a plane headed to Houston. Will arrive 2:17 p.m. Working on a case in southeast Texas somewhere. Call me on my cell phone. Hope to hear from you. I miss you."

Lucas Tanner and Mel met in California at a Christmas boat parade party several years earlier. Lucas had something to do with oil fields and equipment and rarely stayed at his Houston home base. She worried for his safety. He and his crews worked around the world and had been recently under missile attacks in Baku during a heated political crisis. Although this long distance relationship was tenuous at best, they'd soon become long distance lovers.

Her plane landed through low gray clouds at George Bush International Airport north of Houston. Mel grabbed the first rental unit she could find, turned on her global positioning satellite (GPS), and typed in Z-a-v-a-l-l-a. The GPS suggested two routes: Interstate 10 eastbound through Beaumont, or a smaller Highway 59 northbound. Might as well take the interstate she knew well, as it linked commercial traffic from California to Florida and while well-traveled, might be the faster route. She knew I10 better between Los Angeles and Palm Springs where she often visited desert friends.

Heavy rain pelted the blue-black rental car. The washers squeaked and made long streaks often leaving water on the windshield. Mel turned on the defroster and wiped the inside of the windshield as she slowed, moved to the right lane between two eighteen-wheelers, and followed them into Beaumont.

The storm raged, and lightning lit the afternoon sky. Thunder drummed the air that surrounded the car. The noise startled Mel. The radio weatherman called it, "A real gully washer."

Her cell phone rang.

"Where are you?" Johnnie asked.

"I must be in Texas. Can you hear what's playing on the radio?"

"Not so clear. What is it?"

"She Thinks My Tractor's Sexy."

Johnnie laughed. "Hey, that's my favorite country dance number. Talk about sexy; did you connect with Lucas yet?"

"No. I left a message on the recorder. I'm not sure if he's even in the country right now. Say, did you get anything on Boudreaux?"

"Good stuff in California, and I'm cooking the computer for criminal links in Texas and Louisiana."

"Shoot."

"Got four to seven years for burglary and three arrests for domestic abuse. Also, has two outstanding DUI warrants."

"That's not surprising. Any info on the burglary?"

"Yeah. He worked on the cash register, a day shift, at a service station combination mini-market in Huntington Beach. The manager suspected one of his twelve shift guys was stealing from the till."

"Uh, huh."

"He asked them to take lie detector tests, but all twelve declined."

"Doesn't that give you a warm fuzzy feeling?"

"Yeah. Anyway, the owner set up hidden surveillance cameras in the walls and under the counter with the lens directed at the cash register and the safe drop."

"What's a safe drop?"

"To prevent losing large sums of money in a robbery, the store has an iron clad rule that when $300 is collected, the money is placed in an envelope that is dated, stamped, sealed and dropped into a slot in the top of the floor safe."

"Keys?"

"No employee had a key, and that information is posted on signs at the front doors."

"And they caught Boudreaux?"

"Only him and in Technicolor. Both cameras caught Henry Lee removing cash from the envelopes before sealing them. Also, he was putting someone else's initials on the envelope."

"Nothing about him carrying weapons?" Mel asked.

"Nothing yet, but be careful. It's legal to carry a gun in Texas, and I suspect he owns a couple, at least."

Chapter Five

As Mel neared the town of Zavalla, the storm clouds moved past; and Mel pressed on the accelerator to make up for lost time. A succession of three signs about fifty yards apart read: a seventy mile per hour speed zone, then Zavalla city limit, pop 701. Following that, she saw a thirty-five mile per hour city speed zone sign. A wood-pulp truck barreled down on her rear bumper, so Mel tapped her brakes slowing her speed to only fifty-five. At least that's what the cop told her when he asked for her identification a few yards past the city limit sign.

"May I see your driver's license, registration, and proof of insurance?"

Even with his soft drawl, that sentence is clear in any dialect.

The officer's uniform shirt strained at the belt line. His Texas star belt buckle shined. Paul Ames, Marshall, Sheriff appeared on the name badge pinned across his heart.

Mel handed him the rental agreement, then reached into her wallet and withdrew her license to which she had previously clipped a crisp $50 bill. She handed the packet to the sheriff without a word and waited.

He pushed his hat back revealing a full head of white hair, "Someone in Cal-e-forn-e-ia tell you that bribery walks tickets in Texas?"

"Actually, that's my mad money that I keep for emergencies."

"Is this an emergency?"

She stared out the windshield. "You tell me, Sheriff."

He didn't answer her for a few seconds. "Camellia Walker. Anybody call you Mel?"

"Everyone who knows me."

"Yore daddy a cop?"

Mel jerked her head around and looked into his deep gray eyes. "Yes-s-s," was her cautious reply.

"My sister told me you'd be coming to town." "Is your sister a clairvoyant?"

"No, she's a battered woman."

"Dee is your sister?"

"Yep."

"Why'd she ask me to get involved in Angel's case if her brother's in law enforcement?"

He leaned in toward the driver's door. "I asked her the same question."

"I'd like to know her answer."

He stood erect again. "Ma'am, it's a family thing."

"And none of my business?"

"You got it. Now Ca--, uh, Mel, why don't you follow me to the courthouse, and let's get this speeding ticket taken care of? Then you should have enough time to catch the next plane for L.A. before dark."

"You're going to give me a speeding ticket?"

"Fifty-five in a thirty-five, plain as day."

"You can't slow from seventy to thirty-five in one-hundred

yards with a truck loaded with trees smoking up your tailpipe," she argued.

"Tell it to the judge." He pulled his police car around in front of her and turned off the light bar. She switched on the ignition. The lack of a roaring engine was replaced with the sound of a dull click, not that of a healthy motor.

The sheriff pulled onto the highway and drove for half-a-mile before realizing Mel wasn't behind him. He spun the car around on the wet pavement, leaving skidding sounds and smoking tires and raced toward her. He put on his light bar, as he pulled alongside.

He jumped out of the unit gripped a flashlight in one hand and his still-holstered gun in the other. "I told you to follow me. Are you trying to be cute?"

"I'm trying to start the car. She put both hands in the air, palms out. It won't start."

"Pop the hood."

The afternoon sun played hide-and-seek behind the tall pines that lined the road. Clouds from passing rain shrouded the two-lane highway into a shadowy mist. He turned on the flashlight.

Mel waited for his cue.

"Now turn the ignition."

She did.

Nothing.

"Did you hear me, Ma'am? Turn the ignition."

"I did. Several times."

"Not even a click. Battery looks okay. No belts broken."

Several minutes passed. The sheriff had removed his white ten-gallon hat and scratched his white hair. Mel used her cell phone and called the rental agency.

"My car won't start."

"Got any idea why?" The female voice asked.

"If I knew, why would I call you?"

"Where are you, Ma'am?"

"Zavalla."

"Where's that?"

"Southeast Texas, north of Beaumont and Vidor."

"Just a minute, please," and music filled the earpiece followed by an advertisement about their fine dependable service."

"They have me on hold," Mel told the sheriff.

He slammed the hood shut, directed traffic around both cars, and set out flares.

"Ma'am?" A new southern voice drawled, "Can I help you?"

"This is Camellia Walker, and my car won't start."

"Where are you?"

"I just told the other lady, I'm in Zavalla."

"And that's...?"

"In southeast Texas, north of Vidor and Beaumont." She screamed into the mouthpiece.

"Ma'am, you don't have to be rude. I just asked a simple question."

"Listen, fella. I've already told this story to another person. I'm in a 701 person town, with a traffic ticket, a small town sheriff, flares, and a rental unit that won't start. It's getting late, and I'm tired. Just bring me a new car."

"Hold the line, please," he replied, and the recorded message played once more.

Minutes passed when she heard, "Is there a mechanic in that town?"

"Let me ask the sheriff. Sir, is there a mechanic around here?"

"Sure, we got a mechanic."

"Great. Yes, Zavalla has one."

"So, it's getting late here, too late for us to come fix the car. Get towed to the shop and have him call us after 9 a.m. tomorrow with his estimate."

"You can't deliver another unit?"

"Not tonight. We're short of help. Jake's off; he just had twins. Betty Sue's on sick leave, pneumonia, I think..."

"Listen, fella, I don't care about your personnel problems, except that you're making them my problems."

"Listen here, little lady. Have the guy look the car over and give us a call tomorrow. It's that simple. For now, get a good night's sleep, and you'll feel better. Good night."

"What'd he say?" the sheriff asked.

"For us to have it towed and ask your mechanic to call him with an estimate tomorrow."

"Can't do that?"

"Can't do what?"

"Have it towed."

"Why not?"

"Slim's fishing."

"Who's Slim?"

"The mechanic."

"Why didn't you tell me that?"

"You didn't ask. You asked, 'Do we have a mechanic?' We do. It's Slim, and he's fishing."

"Until?"

"He's all fished out."

"You gotta be kidding me."

"Listen here lady, that sarcasm might work in California, but your tone won't get you anywhere in Texas."

Mel took a deep breath and exhaled. "Will a better attitude get me a ride to a hotel?"

"What hotel?"

"Where visitors stay."

"Visitors stay with family. Other people got no business here. They stay away."

Mel's heart pounded in her chest.

"How close is the nearest hotel?"

"Back in Beaumont or north to Lufkin, but you'd need a car to get there."

She pounded the steering wheel in desperation. "So, what do we do, Sheriff?"

"Grab your bags, lock the car, and let's go for a ride."

A few miles north they parked in front of a two-story white brick building that was dark save for one light on the lower floor.

The sheriff motioned for her to follow him. The front door was unlocked, and he held it open for her, then pointed her toward the lighted room.

He knocked on the door, waited a respectful period, then pushed the door open and walked in. His boots made clicking noises on the worn hardwood floors as he directed her to a chair. A man who could have been the sheriff's twin sat behind a weather-beaten wooden desk. His name plate caught her eye.

Judge Marshall.

"Any relation?" She asked.

"My brother," the sheriff replied, as he tossed the ticket copy in front of the judge.

Mel waved a finger between the men. "You two don't see any conflict of interest here?"

The men looked at each other and smiled. That was her reply.

The judge spoke. "So, Miss...ah, Walker fifty-five in a thirty-five?" He picked up a pencil and with the eraser end pushed on the numbers of a hand-held calculator.

Good grief, she thought. *Will they take a credit card?*

After several restarts, he hit the total button, pulled his reading glasses from atop his balding head setting them squarely on his nose and leaned forward. "The grand total is four hundred and fifty dollars."

Mel's mouth dropped open.

The sheriff spoke. "Oh, and her rental car is stalled near the old cemetery and won't start."

"Oh, so we need to add $150 for each illegal overnight parking, plus," he peered over the top of the granny glasses, "what you think Slim will charge for towing?"

"He's fishing," Mel answered.

"Oh, all right. Then we'll let him handle that when he gets home. So, say $600, and we'll call all this even. Tonight," the judge said.

"Say I post ten percent bond which is about all I have in cold cash, and we'll call it even until I can hire a lawyer?"

"How 'bout our Sheriff Paul Ames Marshall taking you to our hotel for the night, and we'll clear this up in the morning?"

Mel stood and grabbed her purse. "I thought you said you didn't have a hotel here."

She followed Sheriff Paul Ames Marshall up a narrow stairway where he flipped on a single light illuminating two small jail cells.

He said, "Take your choice."

Without any argument, she entered one. He slammed the metal door behind her, shut off the light, and left the room not saying another word.

Chapter Six

The windowless cell kept the night coolness at bay as Mel found toiletries, clean sheets, a blanket, and a pillow on the cot. She made a bed, brushed her teeth in the wash basin, and slept hard after an exhausting day.

The sound of a ringing cell phone brought her to consciousness the next morning.

Johnnie's cheery voice said, "Good morning."

"Yeah?" Mel replied, rubbing her eyes and stretching.

"Where are you?"

"In jail."

"Wha...?"

"Don't ask."

"You've just been gone one day, Mel. Do we already need bail money this morning?"

"Probably." The smell of coffee and bacon caught her attention. "But it looks like I don't need breakfast. I think it's here."

The jail door opened and a petite brown-haired teenager pushed in a tray. "Good morning. Welcome to Zavalla," she said.

"Oh yeah, I can tell you that I'm thrilled to be here."

"Who's that?" Johnnie asked.

"The welcome wagon with breakfast. Can I call you back in a few minutes when I get the new bad news? Last night the number was $600."

"Ouch. What'd you do, kill someone?"

"No. But don't give up on me. I might yet. It's a long story."

"Take care, Mel. Call me right back. I'm at the office."

"Bye."

Mel stood and looked into the greenest eyes as the girl ducked her head, sat the tray on the edge of the cot, then backed out of the cell and locked the door behind her.

"Thank you. It smells wonderful." Mel gripped the coffee pot to warm her hands. "My name's Mel."

"I'm Gina Gribow Thompson," she said, making no eye contact with Mel.

Mel sat on the cot's edge and buttered her toast.

"Did you cook this for me?"

"No, my Mama did."

Mel wolfed down the bacon, eggs, and toast, but passed on a small white grainy pile of what appeared to be minced rice smothered in butter.

"You don't like grits?" Gina asked.

Mel pointed, "You mean this? I've never eaten grits."

"Foreigner," Gina said, as she turned and left the jail area.

After the third cup of coffee, an urgent call of nature kicked in.

"Hello out there. Gina, I need help."

Sheriff Marshall popped his head in the door. "Gina's gone to school. Whatcha' need? Potty time?"

"How'd you guess?"

Mel re-brushed her teeth with a small travel bag provided

by the City of Zavalla, combed her hair, and walked toward the cell area as the sheriff sorted through the morning mail.

"Have a seat." He motioned to a captain's chair across from his desk.

"Thank you."

A small package wrapped in grocery bag butcher paper and tied with two dirty white shoelaces lay on the desk at the bottom of the mail stack. The sheriff took a small pen knife from his pants pocket, cut the strings, and tore back the brown paper from the shoe box.

"One thing we need to get straight right here and now, little lady. You gotta pay your fine this morning. We'll get your car fixed; then you gotta go home. This Angel Boudreaux business is hometown business. She's my niece. I'll find her. No fancy California cop 'wannabe' is going to tell us how to conduct this investigation."

He had a way of pronouncing California that made Mel's blood pressure rise. "My name is Mel, and I have a client and a responsibility to this missing child. My father was a cop. He was murdered. I have no desire to be a cop. I am an investigator. I didn't ask for this assignment, but now that I'm here, I have a job to do. I'm not leaving without Angel."

He wadded the paper, dumped it into the trash, cut the sticky tape, and removed the lid. Inside, waxy paper covered the view to the bottom of the box. He lifted it up. "Jesus Christ." Sheriff stepped away and covered his mouth and nose.

A pungent odor, like decaying flesh, filled the small area. Mel recognized this smell.

She stood and looked inside. "Don't see many body parts in this area, do you?"

"Jesus, what is that?" He asked.

"It's a small organ of some kind. You got a coroner around here? A doctor? A medical examiner?"

"Yeah. In Lovelady, we got an ME out there at the Huntsville prison unit."

"Let's go," Mel said, as she picked up the box with its contents, grabbed her purse, and walked to the door.

The Lovelady Unit covered an open flat area in the middle of the East Texas piney woods. On prison grounds and for miles as they approached the unit, peas, corn, hay, and beets had been carefully planted in straight rows and were being harvested by chain gangs of prisoners. The men wore orange uniforms, boots, and were shackled together in groups of five. Each had a hoe, rake, or a burlap bag. They worked without looking up. Mel noticed there were no tall electrified fences anywhere in sight. She pointed at the scene and asked, "What keeps them from running away?"

"See those horses there?"

A number of guards on horseback, each wielding a long rifle, with a bloodhound by their side, surrounded the group of the harvesters.

"Yes."

"No man on earth gonna outrun a horse, a bullet, or a dawg hell-bent on dinner."

"Gotcha." Mel nodded.

They approached a tiny guard house and stopped behind a car. "Everybody gotta get out of their car before reaching the unit."

"Okay." Mel held the package on her lap and prepared to exit when their time came.

The guards looked under the hood and in the trunk of the lead car. As the sheriff drove up, he slowed, waved, and drove through.

So much for rules, Mel thought.

Several miles down this one-lane graveled road, the prison buildings came into sight. The sheriff followed signs to the administration building parking area and stopped.

"We're here to see Doc." He told the uniformed man at the front desk.

An older man, who reminded Mel of her family doctor, walked through a set of security doors wearing a short white lab coat and dried his pale white hands on a paper towel.

"Hey, Paul Ames. How's the Sheriff business coming along?"

"Fine Doc. This is Mel. She's an investigator from California."

They shook hands and exchanged greetings.

"Whatcha' need today?"

"We got a body part. Mailed to me at the jail. You got time to take a look at it?"

The doctor smiled, "Always have time for a body part." He motioned for them to follow him through the metal doors, down a short hallway, and into a large sterile morgue. He pulled a set of rubber gloves from an open box, snapped them on his wrists, and took the box from Mel. He walked it to the shiny metal table, pulled down a large round light, and removed the shoe box lid.

At that moment, the white metal doors flew back; and an attendant pushing a covered gurney rolled into the room. Mel jumped. Even the sheriff grabbed for his sidearm, then laughed.

"Hey, you scared me." The sheriff said.

"How ya doing Paul Ames?" The man asked.

"We're fine. Bobby Gene, this is Mel Walker. She's an investigator from California. Mel, this is my brother Bobby Gene."

Mel extended her hand. Bobby pulled off a latex glove and shook her hand.

"Geez, Sheriff. How many brothers do you have?"

"Too many. And those are just the ones we know of."

Everyone laughed at this Texas humor.

"Howdy, Mel. What brings you to Texas?" Bobby Gene asked.

"Our sister Dee Dee asked her here to help find Angel." Paul Ames replied.

"Why would Dee Dee do that?" Bobby Gene offered this question to the group.

Mel answered. "Why indeed?"

"Beats me," Sheriff replied.

Bobby Gene pointed to the box. "What's that?"

"That's what we're here to find out," Mel responded.

The coroner reached in the open box and withdrew the pink and gray spongy pulp that dripped with fluids. He turned it over in his hands, pushed his bifocals back on his nose and said, "Hmm."

Neither Mel, the sheriff, or Bobby Gene spoke while the doctor took a small scalpel and scraped a section, placed it on a slide, and examined it under the microscope.

"Well?" The sheriff paced back and forth.

The doctor looked first at Bobby Gene, then to Mel and the sheriff. "What you got here, it's just a spleen." He fished with his fingers through the tissue and bloody goo that remained in the bottom of the box. He then added as he pointed one hand in the air with a wet drippy ring trapped on the tip of his pinky finger, "And this here's a high school ring."

Chapter Seven

"Could this spleen belong to a once healthy little girl?" Mel asked.

"Could. I need to do more work. I'll call you later with a report."

The ashen-faced sheriff staggered off balance against a cabinet and supported himself on a door handle. "Oh, my God, my niece, Angel, is missing, Doc. Treat this as a crime scene. Document everything. Damn, if this is Angel's spleen, I'll kill that SOB." He turned to Mel.

"Forget it," Mel said. "You can arrest me if you dare, but short of tar-and-feathering, I'm not leaving town until I have Angel."

"Jesus," was all Bobby Gene could say, as he rolled the covered corpse past them and into a storage room beyond the morgue.

"Mel, we don't do that anymore. But if this is her organ, we got a major crime..." His voice trailed off as he wiped his eyes with a cotton handkerchief.

"First, let's go back to the office, and you take my fingerprints so we can eliminate mine from the box and paper. Let's get the postal carriers prints and yours too." Mel said.

"I told you..."

Mel interrupted, "And I told you. I'm not leaving without Angel. I made a promise." She turned to leave and spoke directly to the physician, "Honestly Doc, I don't know why you'd even get in this line of business."

"Well, Mel, in all sincerity, I like working with people."

News about the spleen spread through Zavalla. By noon, anyone who might have touched the box had been fingerprinted.

"Whoever did this wasn't very imaginative," Mel said.

"Yeah. The shoe box is postmarked Zavalla. That gives us 700 suspects, excluding myself."

"Assuming it wasn't just someone driving through town. Say, you don't have a forensic department here, do you?"

"No. We'll have to give the box and all our fingerprints to the Texas Rangers. They have a crack crime lab. Most times the crime gets solved at the Ranger lab without us having to send stuff to the FBI's lab in Virginia."

"What about the ring?" Mel asked.

Sheriff Marshall turned the ring over and remarked, "It's from Beaumont Charlton Pollard High School, class of 74." He squinted, bringing the ring to his face. "The initials are HLB. That low-life bastard."

"Who?"

"Henry Lee Boudreaux, Angel's dad."

"Are you sure? Would the year be about right?" Mel asked.

"Yeah. He's been gone from here off and on for about ten years. He married Dee right out of high school. Angel was born a couple of years after that."

"Damn. Do you know where he is?"

"Oh, he's got family here, near Boudin Lake. We try not to bother them. They're just plain trash. Drunks, drug addicts, all inbred. Nasty situation. Got kids, dawgs, and chickens all running around loose with no sense. None of them."

"My kind of people. Sounds like a good place to start. Since I don't have a car, want to drive me there?"

Sheriff Marshall started to object but realized he was outmatched.

They turned off the highway and left the asphalt behind. The deeply rutted sandy road caused the four-wheeler to bottom-out several times. Overgrown bramble scratched both sides of the vehicle, and mud splashed from the ruts as a light mist settled in around them. A chill accompanied the haze.

Homemade and misspelled NO TRASSPASS signs, spaced about every hundred feet, appeared on fence posts.

"How far do they live off the main road?" Mel asked.

"Far enough to have these warning signs, a lookout, and several rifles aimed at us right now." He turned on the light bar, hit the siren twice, and slowed to a stop. Three barefooted men wearing bib overalls stood in the middle of the rough road.

He rolled down the window and called out. "Now, Boudreaux, put that rifle down. It's just me and a visitor from California. A friend of Dee's here wants to talk with you."

The men motioned for Mel and Sheriff Marshall to exit the vehicle. He shut the engine off; they stepped out of the car with both their hands in the air and walked slowly toward the men.

Mel spotted a brown furry animal hanging from a nearby pine tree, its entrails neatly cut away, with blood pooling in a jug at the foot of the tree. "Is this deer season?" Mel asked in a whisper.

The sheriff raised his voice to answer. "This isn't deer season. It isn't doe season either, and Boudreaux thinks that's why we're here. But we ain't here about that doe, Boudreaux. I expect you heard Angel is missing."

"I heard."

"This is a friend of Dee's. She asked her to help find Angel and make sure she's safe."

The man who appeared to be Boudreaux spoke again. "We don't need no help finding Angel. Everything's all right here."

Mel said, "I'm not leaving..."

But Sheriff Marshall interrupted her, "Now, Mel. This is man's business. Remember your place."

Mel put her hands on her hips, "This isn't the 50s boys, and it isn't just man's business. I have a job to do. I spent last night in jail. I have no car. I've had no bath today. I'm hungry and very irritated right now. My father was a cop, so those rifles don't scare me. Now don't any of you piss me off."

Two of the men chuckled. The sheriff's mouth fell open. Boudreaux lowered the rifle to his hip and spoke. His South Texas accent sounded like honey flowing over his vocal cords. "We all been in jail. We ain't got no car, and we ain't washed in weeks. That's no big deal ma'am. Come on up to the house, and maw'll get you some coffee and a biscuit."

They left the police unit behind and followed the men through the woods to what only could be described as a cabin made from scraps. Wood, metal, shingles, siding pieces, hubcaps, and aluminum pieces had been nailed to all sides of the house. A small porch had been built using broken pallets stacked on top one another as a stoop.

Boudreaux dismissed the other two who walked into a small shed nearby and began shoveling hay into a wheelbarrow.

He called out, "Maw, bring some coffee and biscuits out here. We got visitors."

A woman carrying two cups of coffee stepped through a screen door that squeaked when she opened it. Mel's first impression of Mrs. Boudreaux was that she was a fifty-year-old, gray-haired, haggard female. Years of bad decisions rolled down her face even when she grinned her toothless smile.

Mel returned the smile. "Good afternoon, Mrs. Boudreaux. Thank you." Mel took the dingy cup and left the biscuit on a dirty plate. The woman's grimy fingers and broken nails spoke volumes about the importance of good hygiene and monthly manicures.

The sheriff drank from his cup. Mel didn't.

He spoke first. "We need to talk to Henry Lee. Got any ideas where he is?"

The woman returned to the house without a word.

"Nope. Ain't seen him in weeks, maybe months." The man scuffed one worn boot toe against a small rock in the sand. "Nope."

He shook his head but gave Mel no eye contact. Her FBI polygraph friend had trained her that was one mark of a liar.

"Any idea where we might find him? Or call him?" Mel asked.

"Nope. None our folks got a phone."

"Have you seen Angel?" Sheriff Marshall asked.

"Nope. Last I heard she was in school in California."

The thick mist settled into the small clearing around them. The birds quit chirping. A dog howled in the distance.

"Well, if you see or hear from Henry Lee, ask him to contact me," Sheriff Marshall said, as he tossed the coffee grinds against a nearby tree and sat the empty cup on the pallets. Mel followed suit. "Thank the Misses for the coffee."

As Mel and Sheriff Marshall drove away, Mel asked, "Was that Henry Lee's brother?"

"Yeah. 'Bout as worthless as Henry Lee, too."

"What's his name?"

"Brother."

"And his wife's name..."

"Sister."

"I had to ask didn't I?" She chuckled. "Do you think we'll hear from them?"

"Nope. But, even without a phone, they'll spread the word that we're looking for Henry Lee and Angel."

"Where will that get us?"

"Probably nowhere, but I thought I'd scare them a bit."

"Oh yeah, we scared them all right."

"No harm making our presence known. They never seen a strong woman like you."

"We probably should get back to the station so I can have some money wired to me to pay the fine. Where am I going to stay tonight? I don't want to spend another night in jail."

"We'll talk about the fine later. I know where to find you. Now, about a bed. Let's stop off here."

They pulled into a small graveled parking lot near a white double-wide trailer. *Zavalla City Hall* was stenciled on the door. Inside, several people sat in a large open area chatting. They quit talking and stared as Mel followed the sheriff through the screen door.

"Good afternoon all," Sheriff Marshall said.

"Hey," a few replied, as they changed their position to see Mel better.

An attractive middle-aged woman sat behind the reception desk filing her nails. Her desk was cluttered with envelopes. A computer monitor, adding machine, and telephone completed her work area. Several men in work shirts leaned against two five-drawer filing cabinets. Another sat in a swivel chair sipping a cold drink.

"This is Mel Walker. Dee asked her to help us find Angel."

Mel waved. The response was a cool, "Hey," from several of the men.

"How was breakfast this morning?" the woman asked.

"Great. I met Gina. Is that your daughter?"

"Yeah. She's a good girl, just a little strange."

"Really? She seemed bright to me. The food was so good. Thank you."

"You're welcome. Want a chair?"

"Sure."

One of the men pushed a swivel chair with his booted foot and sent it rolling across the floor. Mel stopped its momentum.

Sheriff Marshall spoke. "We stopped by the Boudreaux's, but they haven't seen Angel or Henry Lee."

A tall, thin young man argued, "They so stupid, wouldn't tell us if they did. The bastards." He stomped out of the room.

"That was Dee's old boyfriend, Roy Allen Ivey. Got kind of a temper, he does. He's had a crush on Dee all his life. He's always been protective of Dee, even after she married Henry Lee," the sheriff said.

"I can see that."

"This is our city clerk and Gina's mother, the Widow Thompson. Over there's our baby brother, Larry Wayne Marshall. And that's my deputy, Charles Lynn Marshall, Larry Wayne's son, who should be out on the highway watching for speeders, not sitting around visiting."

"Hello everyone."

"Sheriff calls me the 'Widow Thompson,' but my friends call me Joanna."

"Hi, Joanna."

"As you can see this town's been run by the Marshall and Thompson families for years. Then the Boudreaux clans moved in and brought lots of trash with them," the sheriff said.

"So you, Dee, Bobby Gene, Larry Wayne, Charles Lynn, and the judge are Marshalls? Do I have that right?"

"Yeah. And Widow Thompson has two sisters, Tiny Opal and Red Opal and their large family. Speaking of which, Mel needs a place to stay for a while. She doesn't cotton to our jail cell."

Joanna picked up the phone, "Let me see if our fishing cabin is available. Hi, Red. We got a visitor in town for a few days. Can we use the cabin? Ah, huh. Okay. I'll get Gina to run some fresh sheets by there after school. You got heating oil? How about some kerosene?"

"I don't want to put anyone out," Mel protested. After hearing the words "Kerosene" and "heating oil, " she wondered if toilet paper or corn cobs would be included.

Joanna shook her head, completed her call, opened a drawer and pulled out something folded and handed it to Mel. "Here's a map."

Sheriff Marshall said, "Honey, her rental car pooped out, so she has no way to get there."

"Slim still fishing?"

"Yep."

"That's no problem. I'll run her by and get her settled in. She can use the work truck for a few days." Then to Mel, she said, "You don't mind putting some gas in and keep an eye on the water level in the radiator, do you?"

"No. That's no problem."

"Well, that's settled."

Joanna grabbed her keys, wrote a short note to her daughter Gina, and motioned Mel toward her four-wheeler in the parking lot. The gray clouds billowed across the sky threatening the day once more.

Mel turned to Sheriff Marshall, "Will you get the fingerprints off to the Texas Rangers?"

"My office already called them. They'll take it to headquarters, and we should have some ID in the next few days."

"Will the doctor have a report on the spleen soon?"

"Soon as he can."

"I pray it isn't a little girl's spleen."

"Me, too, Mel. Me, too. Why don't you get some sleep tonight and drop by my office tomorrow morning? Unless you want to go home. Maybe we can find someone going to Houston, and you can hitch a ride?"

"I don't think so."

"I didn't think so."

Joanna wore blue jeans, work boots, and a denim shirt. Her brown ponytail bounced as she hoisted her small frame into the driver's seat.

"Why did Dee hire you?"

"I don't know. You'd have to ask her. She told Sheriff Marshall about me. But she didn't tell me her brother was the sheriff; her brother was the judge, her brother was..."

"I get it. Sheriff is a tough old codger. No one ever questions his authority here."

"I'll make note of that and not get in his way. I noticed he especially doesn't approve of women in a position either."

"No, he doesn't. Mel this may be the 21st century every-where else in the United States, but we've held to our old fash-ioned values in Texas, especially in Zavalla. A word of caution here, don't make waves. Just sit in the boat and ride along."

"I'd get seasick if I did that."

"What?"

"Forget it."

They drove down a small one-lane road until the pavement ended and continued for several miles through dense brush. The windows were rolled down, and sounds of birds chirped through the haze. The acrid scent of ozone filled the air. A sign informed them they were approaching Boudin Lake.

"Remember when you leave here to make a left turn out of our driveway. Otherwise you'll end up at the dead-end. We're right on the lake. Lots of late night critters, but great sleeping. No phone, no electricity..."

And, no gun, she thought.

Chapter Eight

Joanna pulled the truck into an isolated clearing shared by a small rustic sandstone cabin and several outbuildings. Tall willows, weeping moss, and stately pine trees filtered out much light. Brown pine needles served as ground cover around the cabin.

Mel thought I'm going to stay here by myself with no gun? This could be the end of the road for me. She tried to remain gracious.

"This is quaint."

"Not really. It's damp, because of its proximity to the lake. Critters come visit because they're trying to take their property back. It's dark because there's no electricity."

"And the good part is..."

"For you, it's free, and we're here." Joanna jumped out of the cab, stepped up on the wood-plank porch, and opened the door.

No lock either, Mel thought.

Joanna grabbed a handmade broom inside the door and began dusting cobwebs from the door casing, then swept her way into the shadows beyond. Mel lingered on the porch.

"Think you could walk to Houston tonight?" Joanna called out to Mel.

"You just read my mind."

"Well, you can't. Big storm coming later tonight."

"How do you know that?"

"I can smell it. Can't you?"

"Oh, I smell something all right, but I'm not sure it's rain."

"Once we get a fire going this place will be cozy as a bug in a rug."

"What kind of bug?"

"Crickets, chiggers, water bugs, lightning bugs, oh, and a couple of moccasins might mozzy on through on their way to the lake."

"Snakes?"

"They won't bite you. Just use the broom and sweep them through the cabin."

In the next hour, Joanna gave Mel a grand tour of the two-room cabin, taught her how to gather firewood, stack and start a fire using a long match and the back side of one's denim jeans, pump water from the well house, hot-wire a GMC truck parked in one of the sheds, and most important of all, a lively demonstration on the honeypot vis-a-vis the outhouse.

Joanna jumped off the plank porch. "Don't worry about cooking dinner. Come into town before seven, and Tiny Opal'll feed ya. The rest of Zavalla will probably be there to take a look at you anyway."

"How will I find her?"

"Jimmy will take you right to her diner."

"Jimmy who?"

Joanna pointed to the GMC. "Jimmy."

"Oh, the GMC. Gotcha." Mel thought I'll never speak Texas, much less understand it.

As soon as the sputtering of Joanna's truck's engine faded through the forest, a damp stillness filled the void. One by one noises began. Noises Mel never heard before. One sounded like a woman being strangled. She unpacked her suitcase, put another log on the fire, and boiled a kettle of water for chamomile tea.

The roar of the fireplace fought against the air's chill. She shivered, then added a windbreaker to her body layering. The tea warmed her insides, and she snuggled into a down blanket on the sofa and promptly dozed off.

You know, sometimes when you're alone, then aware somehow that you're not — alone that is?

Chapter Nine

That's how Mel startled herself back into consciousness.

She jumped to her feet and in an instant decided to use the blanket as her defensive tool. She tossed it over the intruder's body and wrestled the wriggler to the ground. She smothered the person, sat straddle-legged, and bound flailing arms to their sides with her knees.

A female called out. "Let me up. Let me up." Her head bobbed up and down, slamming it against the wood flooring.

Mel continued sitting across the body binding it to the floor. "Who are you? What do you want?"

"It's me, Gina Gribow Thompson. Let me up."

Mel stood and pulled away the blanket. Gina crawled to her feet and dusted herself off.

"I'm sorry. Are you all right?"

"I'm fine. Sorry I startled you."

"How'd you get here? I didn't hear any vehicle?"

"I'm a shadow. I walked quietly over the dew and through the woods."

"What are you doing here?"

"I bought you something." Gina took off her backpack, unzipped it, and removed a package wrapped in a towel. "Here."

Mel unrolled the towel to find a Smith and Wesson, an extra clip, and a box of bullets. "What a lovely, yet personal gift. Think I'm going to need it?"

"You might. You might not. I'd feel better if you had it."

"Me too. Is it registered?"

"According to the Second Amendment to the U.S. Constitution ratified in 1791, 'the right of the people to keep and bear arms shall not be infringed.'"

"Is that a 'No?"

Gina stood mute and stared at the fireplace.

"That was not my question. Registered is not infringed." Mel stood with the gun in one hand, the other on her hip. "Besides, I have the Jimmy. Doesn't it have a gun rack?"

"Yep, but there's no gun in it." Gina turned around, slung her backpack between her shoulder blades and walked out the door. "You're welcome. Don't ask, don't tell. Especially my mother. She worries. I'll pick it up from you when you leave town." She left without another word.

Mel folded the blanket, had a second thought and ran to the door to call after her, "Gina, I'm going into town. Want a ride?"

Gina was nowhere to be seen.

The cell phone rang, and Mel scrambled back into the cabin to retrieve it.

"Please be a happy voice," she said.

Crackling noises filled the earpiece.

Johnnie hollered, "I'd be happy if I could hear you clearly. Can you hear me now?"

"Barely. This is the best we can do. I'm deep in a forest in the middle of nowhere."

"Sounds like."

"Whatcha got for me?"

"I need you to come home. Right away."

"What's the matter? Are you all right?"

"I'm fine. And I'll be much better when you're home. There's a lot of work to be done here."

"I thought you wanted me to find Angel."

"I was wrong. Let's let the police do their thing."

"Oh, now I know something's wrong. We never let the police do their thing. Give it up."

"Listen, Mel. This Henry Lee is no one we want to mess with."

"Because..."

"I called Jack over at the FBI. He called a friend at the Texas Ranger's office, who talked with the Beaumont police who..."

"Okay, okay, he called, she called. I got it. Get to it."

"Despite their best efforts, they don't have a good body count on the number of people that have entered Henry Lee's life and are now missing and presumed dead."

"Guess."

"Twenty to twenty-five seemed to be a consensus."

"That's an impressive number."

"Men, women, and children."

"Wow."

"There's one very interesting story about a former wife and her lover whose body parts floated..."

The reception began to fade.

"I can't hear you," Mel hollered.

"Are you alone?" Johnnie asked.

"As I can be."

"Give me the phone number there. I'll call you back on a landline."

"There is no landline."

"Give me the address, lock the door, and stay inside. I'll contact an investigator in Houston right away and have them come get you."

The phone beeped several times, then died.

"Oh yeah, I'll be sure to lock the damn door," Mel yelled, as she threw the phone into her suitcase and sighed

After stoking the fire, her warmth returned. She checked the gun for bullets, pulled on her jacket, then dropped the gun into her purse, grabbed a flashlight, and crossed the small clearing to the GMC. In no time at all, Mel connected the correct wires, and the truck engine chugged to life. That she was destined to a life of crime occurred to her when the engine turned over and purred. She double clutched, changed gears, and bounced down the rutted road to dine with the city of Zavalla.

Mel asked to use the diner's wall socket to recharge her cell phone while she and several members of the Thompson and the Marshall families joined her for a carbo-rich dinner that ended with homemade peach cobbler. She found herself sitting on a long wood plank redwood table between Bobby Gene Marshall and his brother Sheriff Paul Ames Marshall.

"So, you're a coroner?" Mel asked.

"Well, sort of." Bobby Gene replied.

"Been at this long?" Mel questioned further.

"Long enough to eat dinner and read an autopsy report."

"Me too. Any news on the spleen?"

"Not yet. Whatcha think Sheriff? Couple of days?"

The sheriff replied, "Yeah, a few days anyway."

"My guess is that it's Angel's though." Bobby Gene looked at his plate and stirred the mashed potatoes through the brown gravy. "That's Henry Lee's specialty."

"Body parts?" Mel asked.

"Yep."

"Now, we don't know that for a fact, Bobby Gene," the sheriff interrupted.

"I heard part of one version. What's the official version?"

Mel looked at each man awaiting a reply. Sheriff Marshall spoke first. "Well, for the official version of the crime, Dee Dee is Henry Lee's second wife. His first wife, Terry was a shirttail relative of his, third cousin, by marriage, some such nonsense. Like Dee Dee, every time she stood up, he beat her down. She looked sideways at him; he beat her. I was out there three or four times a week, then he jerked the phone outta the wall, and I quit getting calls from her.

"Couple of weeks go by, and nobody had seen her. Seems the town minister, the very Reverend Sanders, was missing too."

Bobby Gene added to the story, "So, I go fishing one day at Boudin Lake, near where you're staying, and I cast my line, and it snags on something. I pull it in."

Sheriff picked up the story, "Seems two fifty-five gallon drums tethered together and shot full of holes are at the end of his hook."

"So, I drag it to shallow water and pull them ashore. Ooh we, the sun coming up, the stink from the barrels hit my nose. I know that smell."

Mel interrupted, "Death."

"You got it. They was ripe."

The sheriff added the climax, "So, we find body parts in each barrel. Do the DNA, and it's..."

Mel guessed, "The very Reverend Sanders and the very married Terry Boudreaux."

"Right." Both men answered.

Bobby Gene described the gore, "Cut up and gutted like a doe outta season, they were."

Their voices had risen, and the entire table got involved. "Jesus, can you boys leave dead bodies alone for one meal at least?" The Widow Thompson asked.

"I was just bringing Mel up to date on Henry Lee's murders."

The sheriff clarified, "Now, Bobby Gene, we don't know any such thing."

The widow told gossip with a flurry, "Okay, we do know that Henry Lee thought the Reverend and Terry were having an affair."

"'Thought' got nothing to do with it. I saw them," Bobby Gene said.

"You never told me that," Sheriff Marshall said, somewhat surprised.

"Oh yes, I did. I'm sure I did. Jeez, I thought I did. Anyway, they was in the Boudreaux barn doing it. I had bought some hay from them and stopped by there to pick up a couple of bales. They didn't even slow down for me. Reverend kept crying out, 'Holy, holy, holy.' And Terry moaned, 'Oh my.'"

"I never heard that story," Sheriff Marshall said.

"That's so funny." The Widow Thompson laughed.

The sheriff asked, "Did you ever tell Henry Lee? That'd be a great motive for murder?"

"I don't recall I ever did."

The two men began to dispute information gathering and

sharing, and Mel saw that as her invitation to leave.

"Well, this has been a great dinner and lively conversation too, but I have a fire to attend to."

"Be careful driving this time of evening. Lots of wild animals on the road, especially deer."

"Oh, I will and thank you so much for dinner." Mel reached into her purse to pay for dinner, pushing the gun aside and raising the bag high so the sheriff couldn't look directly into it.

"Don't worry about the bill. The county'll pay for it. Just because you're not in jail, doesn't mean we aren't going to keep an eye on you out there. Don't you go too far."

"I won't go anywhere without you, Sheriff. What's next for us?"

Chapter Ten

Morning came early for Mel. She dozed fitfully through the night and grabbed for the gun after each new squawk and peep she didn't recognize. Something jagged and cold pressed into her cheek, causing her discomfort. Even in her sleep, she realized it was a gun. She jumped to her feet and spun around to defend herself against intruders, her hands and arms doing some wild free moves an amateur judo student might do.

"What the hell?" She screamed.

She was alone. She rubbed her sore face and looked in a faded wall-mirror. The cheek imprint of her gun stared back at her.

"Oh, that's cute."

Mel massaged her face until both sides were flush, brushed her teeth using bottled water for rinsing, and combed her hair. Half-dressed in jeans and a long-sleeved shirt, Mel opted for a pair of worn boots she found near the door; and, after pulling on two pairs of socks to make the boots fit, she stepped out into the front yard. A white mist, waist high, rose from the earth's core.

The smell of pine-scented coffee from a nearby fire drew her through the woods. Thick and decaying brush left leaves and spurs on her clothing as she ducked around the concentrated ground cover and waded through the fog toward the lake.

She reached an area surrounded by the tall pine trees that had been cleared of brush and ground cover. In the midst of the semi-circle, a small fire crackled; and plumes of smoke rose up and twirled around the pine needles toward the sky. A black kettle, supported by a metal grate boiled, beckoned her toward both the warmth from the morning mist and the odor of freshly brewed coffee.

"Hello," Mel called out.

Her echo returned.

She walked to the fire and rubbed her hands together, then held them over the fire.

"Don't get burned."

A low male voice startled her, and she spun around.

"Oh, hi Bobby Gene. I hope you don't mind. I'm staying at the cabin," she motioned behind her.

"Yeah, I heard," he said, as he dropped another hand-full of kindling near the fire. "Coffee?"

"Would I?"

Bobby Gene took a blue-and-white speckled cup from his backpack, toasted it over the fire, then poured coffee for Mel.

"Black?"

"Fine."

"Sleep good?"

"No, as a matter of fact."

"Night noises?"

"Yeah."

"Rocks me to sleep."

"It's an acquired taste I assume."

Bobby Gene chuckled. "Want some breakfast?"

Mel rubbed her belly. "Sure. What's on the menu?"

"Fresh bass, jumped right out of the lake, and into the frying pan."

"Wonderful."

"Why aren't you working this morning?" Mel asked as she wiped her hands on her shirttail.

"No bodies, no work. Oh, I also work at the local hospital, but I'm on rotation this week."

"I'm glad you're off." She licked her lips, "I can tell you this is the best fish I ever ate."

"Thank you, Ma'am. We aim to please." Bobby Gene smiled, leaned against a tree, and lit up a cigarette.

"Tell me about Henry Lee."

"He's a bad guy. Anybody disagree with him, poof they're gone."

"Has he always been that way?"

"Yeah, and I've known him practically all my life. He was one evil little dude, always kicking dogs, pouring gas on cat's tails, then setting 'em on fire."

"Was he a bed wetter?"

"Mel, I never knew him that good."

She smiled. "Okay. How about fires. Did he start fires?"

"There was the old plantation barn... but I think that was an accident."

"How old was he?"

"Four or five. Me and him and a bunch of guys was out behind the barn and learning to smoke. Yeah, on reflection, I think that probably was an accident."

"Tell me about his family."

"They all from Louisiana. Mostly red bone."

"Red bone what?"

"That's coon ass for saying they part Indian and part Cajun. Both folks were mad as a bee swarm. Never could hold their liquor. Had a bunch of kids, Henry Lee oldest and meanest of the lot."

"Are they still alive?"

"No-o-o. I don't think so."

"And that means..."

"They been missing about five years, more or less. They pissed Henry Lee off one weekend, threw him out of the house, told him to get a job, take care of his family, bring in some money. I don't know. Probably all those things. Now don't get me wrong. Everybody was drunk after a big city picnic, including me. We drove over there, plopped down on the couch to watch the Cowboys play that Sunday. No reason at all, his ole man came into the living room brandishing his rifle around and ordered us out of there. His ole lady hit us on the heads with both ends of her broom. You should of seen us run. I tripped off the porch, and she whacked me good across my back. Henry Lee got the truck started, and I jumped in the bed as he drove us the hell out of there."

"He didn't have a job."

"Henry Lee makes a living off other people's problems if you know what I mean."

"I'm not sure I do."

"For example, you got a truck that don't work just sitting in the yard. He gets it started and drives it away, so you won't be worried about it collecting dust anymore."

"He steals cars."

"Well..."

"Is this how he supported Dee and Angel?"

"No, they lived mostly on welfare. Then one day, Henry Lee and Dee Dee had a big blow up, and she took Angel and went to California. We have a shirttail relative living somewhere near L.A. Then..."

"We?"

"Dee Dee's my sister."

"Oh, right, I forgot. Anyway, Henry Lee followed her?"

"Then he beat her bad for leaving him. Said 'No one leaves me,' and poof — Angel was gone."

"Why'd you let him get away with hurting your family?"

"That's Dee's business, none of mine. Oh, I tried to talk with her a couple of times. I told her once, 'If you don't like getting beat, you a grown woman, you should take that baby and get out.' She says to me, 'Bobby Gene stay out of my business.' I do."

"That's tough. So, you at least tried."

"You bet and I love that baby like it's my own."

"You have any idea where Henry Lee is? Where might he have taken Angel assuming the spleen isn't hers? For now, I'd like to work on the assumption that she's still alive."

"Henry Lee knows these woods like no one does. He's got caves, old houses, deer blinds, all kinds of places that he could hole up with her. I sure hope you're right."

"Oh, by the way, you didn't happen to see Slim while you were fishing this morning did you?"

"How'd you know Slim?"

"I don't. But I heard he's the only mechanic in town who can fix the rental car I have."

"Nope. Didn't see him. He'll come back when he's fished

out. Like Henry Lee, he knows all the best places too. Pretty much of a loner."

"I was afraid of that." Mel stood and brushed the leaves and dirt from the seat of her jeans. "Well, I guess I'd better plan out my day and get going."

Mel shook hands with Bobby Gene, who waved her on as he cleared the fire pit and stored cooking gear in his pack. By the time she had walked only a few feet into the brush, she turned, but could no longer see the opening, Bobby Gene, or the smoke. Her boots made crackling noises as she walked deeper into the woods humming. She picked up a walking stick and stirred each new bundle of kindling hoping not to see a snake. She hadn't counted on dodging bullets.

Chapter Eleven

The crack of a rifle rang out through the woods. Pellets whizzed past her face catching her by surprise. She dropped to the ground below the white fog and remained still. Despite her fear of snakes and flying, bullets played a strong first on her current fear factor scale.

Shit. Mel remained motionless. A cold chill rose up from the ground and consumed her. She felt light-headed when a sticky substance rolled off her temple toward her eyes. She brushed it away, then smelled it. *Blood. Shit.*

"Mel, don't move," Bobby Gene called out to her.

A rifle shot from another direction shamed the silence. Footsteps pounded the earth getting closer and closer. Mel rose to one knee, with one foot planted firmly, doubled up her fists, and waited for the assault. An arm reached through the whiteness and grabbed her by the shoulder jerking her to a standing position. She swung wildly.

"Hey, wait a minute. It's me."

"Bobby Gene. Jesus, you scared me. Why'd you shoot at me?"

"I didn't. But someone over there did." He pointed through the woods. "The second shot was me. I think I scared him away. You're bleeding. Let's get back to the cabin and have a look at you."

They scrambled around heavy timber growth. Bobby Gene used his rifle to thrash through the underbrush and dragged Mel's hand. Her head spun, temples throbbed, and her throat filled with nausea until she fell exhausted on the sofa inside the cabin.

"Lie still. I'll get your fire going again."

Bobby Gene lit a kerosene lantern and tossed kindling into the fireplace. The cabin soon filled with warmth, and Mel held a wet compress against her head. Bobby Gene pulled the towel away, used a swab with tincture, and touched the wounds. Mel winced.

"Did you get a look at whoever shot at me?"

"Naw, I didn't," Bobby Gene replied. "You know it could have been a hunter who saw movement. You aren't wearing a vest." He motioned to the bright orange vest he wore.

"Sheriff told me it wasn't hunting season."

"Mel. This is Texas. It's always hunting season."

At the sound of an approaching truck, Bobby Gene grabbed his rifle off the kitchen table and ran to the door opening. He peeked around the threshold, then ducked back, and lowered his weapon. "It's Sheriff."

Mel rose off the sofa, held the compress on her head, and joined Bobby Gene.

The sheriff called out, "Is everything all right in there?"

They stepped onto the porch and waved as Bobby Gene replied, "Yeah, we're fine, Sheriff. But someone shot Mel here."

The Widow Thompson, who stood on one side of her truck,

had unloaded a box from the truck bed and walked toward the house. She hastened her steps at the end of Bobby Gene's sentence. "Oh my God, Mel. What happened?"

"Someone took a shot at me."

Joanna Thompson sat the box on the porch and rushed to Mel. "Let me take a look at it."

"Don't fuss over me. Bobby Gene cleaned the wound. It was buckshot. I don't think I'm going to need any stitches."

Joanna lifted the cloth and made a face.

"Is it going to leave a scar you think?"

"Maybe."

"Paul, would you like to run her up to Lufkin to the hospital and let the doctors take a look at her?"

The sheriff, who had been whispering with Bobby Gene on the front porch, entered the cabin and looked at the wound.

"Good grief, I'd had worse things in my eye. It's just a couple of little scalp scrapes."

"It won't ruin my modeling career will it?" Mel asked.

"Not if they photograph you in the dark." The sheriff laughed.

Joanna swatted him with a sofa pillow. "That's not funny." She turned back to Mel. "That's his way of saying you're going to be fine."

"What's in the box?"

"Some supplies. I was planning on bringing them to you when Paul said someone heard gunfire out in this general area. So, he drove along for the ride."

"Is there anything you can do, Sheriff?"

"Naw. The brush is too thick around here. And there are tons of shell casings laying around. No way to match a casing to a specific rifle to this incident."

Bobby Gene added, "No harm, no foul. You're fine, and that's what matters."

"It's probably time for you to get back to California. I could have someone drive you to the airport in Houston if you like."

"You think I'm going to let some coward lie in wait for me and scare me off. Maybe I didn't tell you. My father was a cop. I don't scare easily. And I don't leave cases half done."

"I called Dee. She told me all about you." The sheriff smiled and changed the subject. "The preliminary lab results are in on the spleen. Our fax machine is down. I need to drop by the coroner's office at the prison and pick it up."

"What are the results?" Bobby Gene asked.

"I don't know. The coroner's out of the office, and the secretary isn't qualified to read it."

"Why don't I run by and pick it up and drop it off at the station in a while?" Bobby Gene suggested.

"That'll help a lot. It's probably a good idea to run Mel by the hospital and get her a tetanus shot. No telling whose dirty hands filled that buckshot. We'll meet up later."

"Female Caucasian spleen. Age seven to ten-years-old."

"Damn, I hate that." Mel slumped into a chair.

"That bastard," Bobby Gene said.

"Now don't you two go blaming Henry Lee. We don't know anything yet."

"What do we know?" Mel asked.

"That simple test is just the beginning. We'll need to match the DNA against Henry Lee's type and do an RFLP."

"If we could find him," Bobby Gene said.

"Or Dee's?" Mel said. "She'll be easier to take. We know where she is."

"Right. Now that's thinking it out, Mel. Oh, by the way,

we got the fingerprint report back. Wiped clean. Only your fingerprints, mine, and Bobby Gene's on the box because he picks up the mail for me every day."

"Well, we tried. Can I use your phone to call my office? My cell doesn't work that well out here."

"Sure." The sheriff pointed to his desk and backed away from his chair.

Mel dialed her office. Johnnie's recorded voice left a short message. "Johnnie, it's me. I need you to get Dee by the police department lab for a DNA test as soon as possible. We got some results back on the spleen. The news isn't good, but try not to tell Dee when you work with her. You know what to say without saying it. Have the test results faxed to Sheriff Paul Ames Marshall's attention at this number. Sheriff, what's that FAX number?"

"Mel, it don't work."

"I forgot. Let me give you the prison's FAX number. Send it there for now."

Sheriff opened his file folder and pointed to the prison number, and she repeated it into the recorder and closed with, "Love you Johnnie and don't worry about me. The hospital doesn't think it'll leave any scars, and they gave me a tetanus shot good for ten years."

Chapter Twelve

Mel faked not feeling well and asked the sheriff to drive her back to the cabin so she could rest. She thought that would please him, to do something strong for her when she was so weak. He smiled and hummed the entire drive to the cabin. She was glad to be of service to him, getting out of his way. Anyway, she had things to do and didn't want company or the sheriff interfering.

Bobby Gene's first aid kit lay open on the floor near the sofa. Several wadded wrappers lay nearby along with a couple of antiseptic bottles. Mel heated a cup of hot water over the fireplace, added a stale tea bag, and allowed it to steep. She paced the width of the small room, then paused and stared at the open box anticipating the bandages, tweezers, and scissors might somehow come to life, jump out, and run away.

What could I use to take Henry Lee's DNA, assuming I could find him? She thought. Ah, a cotton swab inside something sterile would do. Oh, yeah, like I'm going to find that in this cabin. But maybe. . .

She leaned over to peek inside the open box. Her cell phone

rang with a high pitch funny-type squeal that she hadn't heard before and that caused her to jump, spilling the tea along the way.

Shit.

"Mel here," she answered.

Static responded.

"Hello, can you hear me?" She hollered.

"Mel? Can you hear me?"

"I can't hear you."

"Who is this? Johnnie?" She screamed as she ran toward the front porch hoping that the open air might improve the transmission.

Static crackled in her ear, followed by silence.

Shit.

Mel sat on the porch for a few minutes listening to the sounds of the forest that were loud and clear, but the phone didn't ring again. She tried dialing her office in California. A recorder told her she was out of the area.

No shit.

She stuffed the phone in her purse and paused long enough before hot-wiring the truck to grab a stick of cotton, a sealed individual bag of tea, and a pair of scissors.

Being the Sacagawea of California investigators, Mel had been to Henry Lee's home once, so she didn't need a map. She turned off the paved highway and bounced through the woods toward the Boudreaux home. She ignored the many handmade "Do Not Trespass" signs and followed the barbed wire fence line to the opening. More junk cars filled the confined area; and the man she knew as Brother Boudreaux glanced up from under the hood of a battered old truck, wiped his hands on an equally dirty rag, and approached her truck carrying a wrench.

"Hi," she said.

"Hi?" He replied cautiously as if trying to place her.

She got out of the truck and walked toward him. "I had a few more questions."

"I got no answers." He turned abruptly, walked back to the truck, and stood on the front bumper ignoring her.

"Would you like some coffee?" A voice startled Mel, and she turned to see Sister Boudreaux's stooped shoulders and down-trodden look as she stood on the pallet porch.

"That's very kind. Thank you, but..."

"She ain't staying that long," Brother called out, as he continued to work under the truck's hood.

"I just ax. Just trying to be hospitable." She shuffled into the cabin.

"We save that for guests. You a trespasser."

"Oh, that's what those misspelled signs meant. I won't stay long; I'd just like to know if you know who shot me this morning?"

"Nope, I don't, and from the looks of it, he wasn't a good shot either."

"Are you a good shot Mr. Boudreaux?"

"Yep, I'm a crack shot." He pulled his torso from on top of the engine and stood in front of the truck. "I only miss on purpose."

"So, that was a warning?"

"Must have been, if they didn't kill you?"

"I want you to know that I'm not going home until we find out if Angel is alive or not, and we arrest her assailant."

"Suit yourself. Not a smart idea."

Mel changed the subject. "Mind if I smell your rifle to see if it's been fired recently?"

"I don't mind telling you; I got lots of guns. They all been fired in the last few days. We need food. We got game."

"But..."

"I guess the short answer is 'No.' Woman, I got no time for your foolishness. Get back to California. This ain't your business." He turned back to his work.

Mel spotted his coffee cup sitting on a split rail fence. She dug into her coat pocket and found a tissue. She snatched the empty cup with the tissue and stuffed it into her pocket, then walked briskly to the truck. "Thanks for your help anyway."

I wonder if I can get DNA from a relative's cup. She thought, as she opened the door of the cab and jumped in.

The radio played country songs while she drove to the main highway. A now familiar sound filled the air. The sound of a rifle round in the near distance.

Chapter Thirteen

Mel pulled into the parking lot in front of Tiny Opal's place next to Joanna's truck. Joanna motioned through the plate glass window encouraging Mel to join her. She removed the coffee cup and napkin from her jacket, set it on the front seat, and entered the café.

"Paul said you haven't been feeling well. Are you okay?"

"I'm fine. The tetanus must have made me a little woozy."

"Coffee?" Tiny Opal called from across the room. "Tea maybe?"

"Sure thing. Want some homemade pie with that?"

"No, thank you."

"Have you been here all your life?"

"Third generation."

"Don't you ever want to take Gina and just get away sometimes?"

"Like to a big city?"

"Yeah."

"Sure. We go into Beaumont for movies all the time."

"No, I mean like Houston, Dallas, Los Angeles."

"No way. Too much crime, traffic, responsibility, people bustling around, always in a hurry. And you?"

"I live south of Los Angeles in Orange County. We have all those things, but I love it anyway."

"You gotta a fella?"

"Sorta. He lives in Houston actually but works around the world. Some oil business thing. How about you?"

"No. My husband got killed in a paper mill accident a long time ago. Gina and me doing fine what with workers comp benefits and my little job."

"You know Paul Ames' crazy about you, don't you?"

Joanna sat stunned in silence.

Tiny sat a cup of coffee in front of Mel and added, "Good grief woman. Didn't you know that? Everybody in town knows I guess, but you and Paul Ames."

Joanna found her voice. "Why Paul Ames and me been friends since we were babies. We went all through school together. Played in sand boxes, attended Sunday school, why Paul and me are..."

"Are what?" Paul asked, one hand on the bench seat.

The ladies had been so wrapped up in conversation they hadn't heard him drive up or enter the café.

Joanna turned beet red. Tiny hustled back to the safety of the counter. That left Mel to break the awkward silence. "Joanna's giving me a little history of Zavalla including your long-time friendship."

"That we have," he said, as he slipped into the booth next to Joanna and patted her hand.

Another embarrassing silence followed. Joanna looked out the window, while Paul put his arm around the back of the booth. Mel spoke first. "So, what brought you here today?"

"I saw your truck and wanted to check on you. How're you feeling?"

"Much better, thank you for asking."

Joanna's stare turned to a smile, "When did you pick up Slick?"

"Slick who?" Mel turned toward the parking lot, pushed out of the booth, and ran out of the restaurant screaming, "NO."

Chapter Fourteen

Mel rested her chin on the window frame in resignation. She sighed as Slick; a one-hundred-pound lab licked Boudreaux's coffee cup. He pushed the cup over and over on the seat, careful not to miss one-inch of the cup with his long tongue.

"That shoots one theory."

Paul and Joanna caught up with Mel. "What theory?"

"I sorta took or appropriated Boudreaux's coffee cup in hopes of pulling some DNA off of it."

"I didn't see you do that," Paul said.

"Oh, not when you and I were there. I went back this morning."

"Alone?" Joanna asked.

"Well, yeah," Mel replied.

Paul grabbed Mel's arm and spun her around. "Never, I repeat NEVER go to Boudreaux's again without me."

"You trying to scare me?" Mel asked.

Joanna looked around to make sure they were alone, lowered her voice, and leaned toward Mel. "Mel, uninvited people, including family members, lots of them, go to that property and are never seen again."

"Even family?" Mel asked.

"Especially family," Paul answered.

"Maybe that's exactly what happened to Angel," Mel said.

"No. I don't think so," Paul said.

"Why is that?" Mel asked.

"They're scared to death of Henry Lee. He's the meanest of the lot," Joanna said.

"Think of the most heartless, most hated Blood or Crips or toughest motorcycle gang member you know. Altogether they don't hold a candle to the hatred Henry Lee has for other people."

Mel clinched the outlines of the gun through her purse. "What are you doing to find him and stop him?"

"The Ranger's sending me a unit. We're pulling a posse together of walkers and horses, and we'll scour this area for him."

"And any possible grave for Angel?"

"Especially that."

"Can you do that without having a warrant for his arrest?"

"Sure. See his daughter's missing, and we found a spleen. For all we know he's in danger of great bodily harm from whoever took Angel. He's a missing person, and we're trying to save his life, make sure he's safe and sound. We wouldn't want anything bad to happen to Henry Lee."

"And that theory works in Texas?"

"You betcha honey. That IS Texas justice."

"Can I help?"

"You can go back to California."

"I don't think so."

"I didn't think so."

By mid-morning a small group of riders, the Explorer Scouts from Lufkin, and a lone Texas Ranger congregated outside the Sheriff's office for instructions.

Sheriff Marshall laid a territory map across the hood of his four-wheeler and using colored markers cordoned off sections as the Texas Ranger issued assignments.

The trackers brought tents, food, and layers of clothing; and each wore an orange vest to warn hunters.

The Ranger wore a white ten-gallon hat, a crisply starched shirt, brown slacks, and freshly-polished cowboy boots.

"Can I ask a question?" Mel said, then added, "Never mind." An adage came to her mind. They sent one Texas Ranger this time because they were looking for only one guy. It's like Texas fighting only one war.

The yapping of dogs drew her attention to the highway as several trucks filled with bloodhounds slid to a stop and stirred dust and pebbles.

The Texas Ranger removed his hat and dusted it against his trouser leg, then walked a few steps toward Mel.

"Hi, I'm Mel Walker." She extended her hand.

"Howdy, Ma'am. I'm Lt. Lamereaux. Call me Bubba."

How'd I know that? She thought. "I don't suppose you're going to let me join the hunt?"

"Can you ride a horse?"

"Ah..."

"I didn't think so." Bubba walked away.

Sheriff Marshall handed Mel a walkie-talkie. "I've got a job for you. You stay here in my office as the coordinator for the riders. As they clear a quadrant, they'll call you for another assignment. Mark this area by group number and the time they called. We'll work till dusk, then bed-down for the night.

Have you heard from Johnnie about Dee's DNA?"

"Nope. I'll call him again this afternoon."

Mel's cell phone worked only slightly better at the sheriff's office than it did from her cabin. After several re-dials, she reached Johnnie's telephone recording and left a cryptic message, "If my cell phone doesn't work, call me at the sheriff's office. We're on a manhunt here." On her office recording she left, "Johnnie did you get the DNA done? Call me." As a last resort, she called Johnnie's cell; and he answered on the fourth ring.

"You got shot?" He hollered into the speaker.

"Well, hello to you too. How're you doing? How's the family? Wish you were here."

"What the hell's happening there?"

"It's a long story. I wasn't wearing orange that day. Just a graze. I'm fine. The tetanus hurt worse than the wound."

"Did they get the shooter?"

"No, really. It was a shooting accident. No harm. No foul."

"Mel, shooters in Texas don't miss. They have guns for teething rings. Come home this instant."

"Wish I could. Got no car. Now you and Rosa got me into this. Now I have a spleen from a seven to ten-year-old female. The Texas Ranger has an all-out manhunt going on. I'm not leaving till they get Henry Lee off the streets."

"Oh, jeez. Any real ID on the part?"

"Is Dee with you?"

"Yeah. You got it."

"Don't tell her about the spleen."

"Are you kidding, of course not."

"Where are you?"

"The FBI called. They broke a ring of kidnappers trying

to smuggle young girls and boys across the border from San Diego through Tijuana. We came down in hopes of finding Angel. The Center for Missing and Exploited Children is coordinating the meeting for us with the FBI."

"Any luck?"

"Not yet."

"Did you receive my message at home?"

"About?"

"I need Dee's DNA so we can match it against that of the spleen."

"Don't you need another side of the family for the match too?"

"Yeah, well, Slick licked that idea away."

"Slick, who?"

"Forget it. You get Dee's DNA, and I'll get another DNA sample here if I have to hunt down and shoot Boudreaux in the ass myself for a sample. And Johnnie?"

"What?"

"Get her sample without alarming her. Okay?"

Johnnie coughed.

"Is your AIDS test current?"

"What's that got to do with anything?"

"You coughed."

"One cough and you rush to prognosis. Of course, it's current and negative. Other than my allergies, I'm fine and behaving, thank you very much for caring."

"Good guy."

"Let me know if you need me then."

"Johnnie, Texas isn't ready for you."

"What? They don't have queers in Texas?"

"Not in Zavalla."

The walkie-talkie made a crackling sound that startled Mel, who had been looking intensely at one of Henry Lee's arrest photos.

"Is everyone in place?" The sheriff asked, and several units responded.

Mel joined them in the parking lot as they paired up and rode off in different directions, just like in a John Wayne movie, Mel thought.

Mel met Gina and Joanna at Tiny Opal's for lunch where Mel regaled Gina with stories of living in "the big city of LA," that included a description of smog, traffic congestion, riots and gang wars, drugs, demonic people, minimum wage jobs, and high-priced real estate. All the while Joanna winked Mel her "Thanks" at discouraging Gina's dream of going to Hollywood and becoming a movie star.

After all was said and done, Gina asked, "If it's that evil, why do you stay there?"

"Because it's all I know. I was born in Huntington Park, a small city south of Los Angeles. It's what I'm used to. Like what you know is the piney woods."

Gina sighed and dredged her french fry through a blob of catsup.

Mel tried to pay for lunch, but Tiny insisted she sign a tab authorized by Sheriff Marshall. She left a handsome tip and decided to retire for the afternoon.

Tiny handed Mel a huge bag. "Oh," Mel protested. "I'm so full I couldn't eat another bite."

"This isn't all for you. It's scraps for Slick and food for you for later. I think he's adopted you."

Mel turned toward the truck, and there sat Slick in the driver's seat. Mel took the bag, and Slick barked.

"Whose dog is he?" Mel asked.

"He's yours now. You should know that no one argues with Slick.

At day's end, Mel turned off the walkie-talkie, dropped it on the floor of the truck cab; and she and Slick drove to the cabin.

A number of patrol cars marked as *Lovelady Prison* units, sped past her, sirens screaming, lights ablaze.

She thought for a small town; they sure did have a lot of police activity.

Little did she know how much.

Chapter Fifteen

Mel lit several kerosene lamps, heated water in a kettle over the fireplace, added kindling and stoked the fire to life. She slipped on a heavy leather glove to tilt the teapot water into her cup. Slick scratched at the door, and she let him out. A few minutes later, he slapped open the door with his paws and stood to look at Mel.

"Well, come on in. I thought you'd go home for the night."

Slick took one step at a time cross the threshold and glanced over his shoulder several times.

"Make up your mind, Slick." Mel stood to close the door behind Slick paced the room's circumference sniffing the rug and scratching at the door cabinet before flopping on a braided rug in front of the fire.

Mel sat on the well-worn sofa, pulled a wool wrap over her lap, and sat mesmerized by the colorful sparks flying around.

She dozed but became aware that Slick's head was erect, his ears high, the hair on his neck bristled slightly, a low guttural growl from deep in his throat rolled over his tongue.

Mel reached for her gun and held it to her chest.

Slick's hair relaxed, and his tail began to wag. He rushed to the door and turned to Mel.

"Who's there?" Mel asked before anyone knocked.

"It's me, Gina Gribow Thompson. Can I come in?"

Mel opened the door. "Sure." Slick jumped up and down several times and licked Gina's hand affectionately.

"Settle down now," Mel urged him only once, and he returned to his post in front of the hearth.

"What are you doing out this late?"

"I told my Mom I'd be here. She said I could spend the night if you guys don't mind."

"What's your vote, Slick?" Mel asked.

He yawned and laid his head between his paws. His tail flicked once and then dropped to the floor.

"I guess that's a 'Yes.' How'd you get here? I didn't hear any engine."

"I'm the Lady of the Darkness. At nightfall, I carry darkness that covers the earth, oh so briefly stopping to visit special paths along my way."

"Okay, whatever." Mel dragged out her thoughts, puzzled by this child's visions. "Why do you want to have a sleep-over with me?"

"I'd like to learn about your exciting career."

"Ah-ha."

"And boys. California boys."

"All right then, child. You are an enigma. Grab a tea bag and a blanket and join me." She patted the sofa. "What I know about California boys shouldn't take too long.

Mel covered guys and their penchants for cars and surfboards, fast cars, and long blonde-haired-bikini-clad girls broken only by Gina's interruptions for clarification.

Gina's interest and experience appeared limited to bull riders, cowboys with large belt buckles, Wrangler jeans, and Alan Jackson songs.

Worlds apart.

"Ever been to Houston?" Mel asked.

"My dream is to go to the Fat Stock Show and Rodeo there. I'm working at odd jobs, and mama says I can go if I earn the money for my round trip bus ticket and some spending money."

"I think you should focus on getting to Houston before you think of California. I'm not sure California is ready for you yet."

Mel's cell phone rang, and they all jumped.

"Hi, Johnnie. I can hear you, but barely."

"Can you hear me now?" He asked.

"Not as good. Walk back where you were. Gimme news."

"I have bad news and more bad news."

"The least of the worst first."

"Angel wasn't in the group of girls the Center located."

"How much worse could it get, Johnnie?"

"Dee refused to take the DNA test, and she's gone."

"What do you mean refused?"

"We drove over to San Diego Police Department's medical lab for the test. I went to the restroom. When I returned, the tech told me Dee said 'No. I can't do this and bolted for the door.'"

"She what?"

"Mel. I've driven around this town for hours and...."

"Jeez, Johnnie. The test is a cotton swab inside the cheek. It doesn't hurt."

"I told her it was non-invasive."

"Did she understand what that meant?"

"I thought she did."

"Why didn't she just say 'No' to the test and hang around?"

"You're asking me?"

"Johnnie. I need that DNA!"

Gina lay asleep on the sofa. Slick's ears unfolded. His neck hair bristled.

"Oh, and one more thing."

"What's that?"

"We may have a Buddy Danko situation here."

Slick jumped to his feet, snarling, snapping, and baring his teeth. The door swung back against the wall with a bang, and a man's voice hollered.

"Hold that dog back before I kill him."

Chapter Sixteen

Mel grabbed Slick's collar and placed her body between the intruder and Gina. She heard Johnnie scream through the static, "Like who?"

The intruder, who wore prison blues, whispered, "Tell the caller goodbye."

She calmly replied, "No need to yell, X-Ray. Just tell Buddy Danko now's not a good time to drop by, unannounced and all. I hope to hear from your people real soon. Bye now." She disconnected.

Slick's barking reached a new shrill. The man kicked at him and warned Mel. "Ma'am, if you don't control your dog, I will kill him."

"He isn't my dog. He's a stray, but I'll try."

Mel found fishing line and knotted one end against the door knob and the other on Slick's leash. "Slick. DOWN. QUIET." She patted his head. He paced back and forth several times stretching the thin leash, then sat on the porch across the threshold and whined a low whimper.

"That's more like it. Are you all alone here?"

Gina answered. "My daddy's out looking for you right now."

Mel got the hint. "My husband's the sheriff here, and he's got a posse out looking for you." Mel moved to the sofa and sat on her gun.

"I need clothes, transportation, and some money."

"Dad's clothes are in town, all except some fishing gear in that chest." Gina pointed to a large quilt box in the corner of the room.

"The Jimmy doesn't work — hasn't worked in years," Mel said. "We're just waiting on Sheriff Marshall right now all right."

Slick snarled, not at all happy with his subjugated role.

The man first tossed through a trunk he found in a closet and kept pointing at them as if his finger held bullets. In the quilt box, he grabbed a flannel shirt and windbreaker jacket and slipped on the black rubber boots Mel had worn the previous day.

"Can I offer you some food? I'll bet you're hungry," Gina asked.

"Food? Yeah, but be quick about it."

"Coffee?" Mel asked as she motioned to the tea kettle hanging above the roaring fire. Mel winked at Gina to get out of the line of fire. Gina moved to the rough-hewn form of a table near the food.

The convict dressed, stuffed his prison blues in the bottom of the chest, stood and turned when Mel drenched his face, head, and chest with scalding hot water from the teapot with one hand and grabbed her gun with the other.

The man screamed in pain and covered his face with his hands. Gina squealed in surprise. Slick joined the duo in a high pitch howl. By the time the noise subsided, Mel pointed her gun at him and shouted, "GET DOWN ON THE FLOOR. DO NOT MOVE."

He moaned and fell to his knees, then to his chest, and spread his arms out to his side.

Mel motioned for Gina to go to the truck. "The walkie-talkie's out there."

Momentarily distracted, the man jumped to his knees and tackled Mel. He landed a hand-chop across her wrist, and the gun spun across the floor in the fray. He pinned her to the ground and pummeled her face and chest, but she got in several good hits before he restrained her with a final fist to the side of her head knocking her unconscious.

He jumped up and seized Gina before she reached the door. Slick strained against the fishing line to no avail as the man closed the door with Slick outside.

When Mel regained consciousness, she struggled against her bonds but realized the convict had tied Gina and her with their backs to each other with heavy-duty rope, as they sat straddled on the wood floor. "What the hell?" was the first comment out of Mel's mouth.

The man finished his cup of coffee and ate from the bag of food that Tiny Opal had given her for Slick. He said nothing, just laughed at them.

She wrestled with the cords as did Gina, but they appeared tight. "Are you all right?" she asked.

"I'm fine. I'm just mad," Gina replied.

"You're more than fine," the convict said. "You're a sweet little thing. I'll bet you're a virgin, ain't you honey?"

Mel wiggled her butt around and tried to kick him with her feet, but he step-sided her and laughed.

He leaned over and touched Gina's long brown hair, "I've been alone a very long time. Ain't been near anyone smelled as pure." He inhaled the fragrance of her freshly-washed hair that he cupped in his hands grimy with food.

Gina screamed at him, "You SOB. You touch me, and my daddy will kill you."

He threw his head back and laughed a noise that Mel could only describe later as "coming from the depths of hell." He lowered the coveralls to his ankles and unzipped his pants, then reached for the zipper on Gina's jeans.

Both she and Mel struggled, twisted, and attempted to turn their bodies against his assault. Mel screamed, "Slick. Come here! Come here!"

The door with no lock rocked open and Slick, whose broken fishing-wire leash trailed behind in the breeze, rushed into the cabin. Slick pounced on the man knocking him to the floor as he twisted in the coveralls around his ankles, unable to stand or roll away from the snapping animal.

The first bite caused a deep shoulder puncture wound, and blood spurted over Mel's face. The man screamed in pain and transferred his attention to the dog deflecting dangerous teeth as the two of them rolled across the wooden floor. Mel felt a release of pressure from her back and moved quickly to rid herself of the loose ropes.

Before Mel stood, she heard a loud BONG, and the man's full weight fell dead across her chest. There stood a smiling Gina holding a black cast-iron skillet with an unconscious convict at her feet.

"Mother always said I should learn to cook."

"You wield a mighty strong swing for a young lady."

"I play on our local baseball team."

"How'd you get loose?"

Gina proudly displayed her pocket knife, "Never know when you're going to need a knife."

"Your mother must be so proud. I know I am. Thanks."

"What are we going to do with him?"

"How are you at hog-tying?"

"I won the championship at the county fair."

"How'd I know that? Okay, let's tie him up with that fishing line, even if we cut off a little circulation. I'll get the radio, and let's find Sheriff Marshall."

In short shrift, they bound the prisoner for delivery. Sheriff Paul Ames Marshall, the Texas Ranger, and his posse arrived in a flurry of bouncing four-wheelers and barking bloodhounds. Slick stood his ground over the threshold and wagged his tail. This was his capture too.

"Are you ladies all right?" the Ranger asked. He ordered the men to remove the bleeding prisoner.

"Oh, we're fine," Mel answered. "Gina's got a knife and a mighty fine swing. Slick, well, he's a hero too."

"We received a call from California from some guy screaming that there'd been an intruder here," the sheriff said.

"Who's Buddy Danko? I heard you say his name," Gina asked.

"A really bad guy who broke into my home once and held me and Johnnie captive. The fella X-Ray that I mentioned is like my brother. He's a local cop."

"Oh, so that was code, huh? That we had a break-in by another bad guy and for him to call the police?" Gina smiled.

"You got it." Mel turned, "That was my associate, Johnnie Blake, who called you. He's working with Dee."

"I didn't know that. How is Dee?" the sheriff asked.

"We don't know right now. We asked her for a DNA sample, and she's missing."

"She's what?" the sheriff asked.

"Gone. Johnnie drove her to San Diego where the FBI had broken a ring of stolen children to see if Angel was among them. Johnnie and Dee had planned to drop by the San Diego PD's crime lab for a mouth swab, but she dumped Johnnie instead. We have no idea where she is."

"Why would she do that?" the sheriff asked.

Chapter Seventeen

"Maybe she isn't the biological mother," Mel said.

"Of course she is. I saw her pregnant as a cow."

"Then, your guess is as good as mine."

Gina tugged on his shirt sleeve, "Did only one convict escape?"

"Yep. That's the guy," the sheriff replied, as he wrapped his arm around her shoulder and gave her a squeeze. "You did a great job, Gina. I'm very proud of you. I should have put you in my posse."

Everyone laughed, but Gina, who blushed at the attention.

The guys loaded up their dogs. Country music blared, opened beer cans spewed, and tires squealed as they sped down the road and out of sight.

"Now, Mel. What are we going to do about this DNA thing?" the sheriff asked.

"I'm wondering since you are Dee's brother if a swab from you might work. Would you give us a saliva sample?"

"Sure, no problem if that would help. However, I don't know that answer. Let's call Doc in the morning and ask him."

"Would Bobby Gene know the answer?"

"I doubt it."

"Gina, ready to go home?" Mel asked.

She turned to the sheriff, "Can I stay the rest of the night? Mom knows I'm here. And now that the guy is in jail, everything should be quiet around here."

"We have Slick to protect us and of course, Gina always has her skillet and her knife."

The sheriff spotted the gun on the floor near the ice chest. He picked it up, smelled it, then asked, "Where'd you get the weapon?"

"Sheriff, I have a 'Don't ask, don't tell' policy. Is that going to be a problem?" Mel responded with a wink.

"Hell no." He laid it on the table, tipped his hat to the ladies, and left.

Gina added fuel to the fire, fed Slick, and she and Mel bundled down for the night. Mel dozed. With only the flickering light from the fireplace, Slick growled a guttural noise deep in his throat.

"Now what?" Mel whispered, as she rolled over and gripped her gun.

Chapter Eighteen

"That's his 'There's a skunk in the area' voice," Gina answered.

"Oh, I feel so much better. What if he stinks up the place?"

"We have some tomato juice in the cabin," Gina replied.

"I don't need a drink, Gina."

Gina chuckled, then rolled over.

Despite the hard cot and her overall weariness, Mel tossed and turned deep into the night. Nearby she heard an owl. A bird responded. Wind rustled through the pine trees, and a coyote howl could be heard in the far distance. An armadillo waddled over the threshold and across the cabin floor, startling her with its shuffle. "What the hell is that?" she asked.

"Armadillo. Ever seen one up close?" Gina replied sleepily from the sofa.

"No. Do they bite?"

"Nope."

"Do they smell?"

"Nope."

"What do they do?"

"Nothing."

"I can't sleep."

"Neither can I."

"Are you hungry or thirsty or something?"

"Hot tea would be good."

Mel stood and stretched. She poured water into the kettle from a large bottle and set the kettle on the hook over the fireplace. She tossed kindling on the fire and wrapped herself up in a blanket on the sofa. Gina grabbed two cups and joined her.

They stared at the fire quietly for a few minutes, then Mel poured. She wrapped her fingers around the mug when Gina spoke. "Want to hear a story about this cabin?"

"Sure."

"Remember the story of the minister and Henry Lee?"

"The one Sheriff Marshall and Bobby Gene told at the café?"

"Yeah."

"Here's what really happened. Henry Lee's first wife, before Dee, was named Terry. Can't remember her last name. I think they were somehow related – distantly anyway, like third cousins. Thibodeaux, or maybe she was a Boudreaux. Anyway, she was a real scag. Rarely bathed. Dirty nails and hair, wore clothes that didn't fit. She didn't care. Never lifted a hand around the house. Didn't cook or clean. What I heard she slept around on Henry Lee."

"If she was so dirty, why would anyone take a chance on disease?"

"Who knows?"

"Ick!"

"We had a minister here named Sanders. Nice enough guy on Sunday morning, but on Saturday night, who-ee. He was a rounder, as my grandmother would say."

"Bobby Gene told me about finding the barrels in Boudin Lake with body parts in them. Were you there when they pulled the bodies in?"

"No, but I came here to the cabin later that morning to see for myself."

"To see what?"

"You ain't much of a country gal are you?"

"Not even."

"Then you don't recognize the slash marks on the front door and why it ain't on hinges or lock, huh?"

"Now, as you mention it."

"Well, folks around here have all their front doors loose, because they use them for cutting boards. They take the door and place it over two saw horses for butchering. Those slash marks are from cutting up animals, like deer and wild pigs and..."

"Terry and the Reverend Sanders?" Mel gulped.

"Yep."

"Jesus. Why didn't they just take the door away and burn it or something?"

"No need to. Folks dead."

"Did they pull some DNA off the door?"

"I don't know what that is."

"A lab takes a sample of the dried blood and matches it to victims to prove that the door was the place of their death."

"Huh. Imagine that. A test. I don't know if they did that."

"How'd you know the killer used this exact door?"

"Because the spirit of the dead comes back here at night sometimes. I hear them sometimes moaning during their love-making."

"What are you doing here alone at night?"

"I wander these woods. You know that."

"And you hear them?"

"I've heard 'em."

"And you're not scared?"

"Not even a little bit." Gina smiled confidentially and laid her head on the sofa.

Mel glanced toward the door. "Well, that story scares the shit out of me."

"You'll get used to it if you stay here long enough."

"Well, as if I needed it, that's good enough reason to speed up my work here."

"Don't like ghosts huh?"

"Not even."

The night filled with noises, but Mel heard no specific moaning as described by Gina. By morning, however, she hustled into action when her cell phone rang.

"Good morning sunshine," Johnnie said.

"Do you believe in ghosts?" Mel asked.

"Of course. Don't you?"

"Not exactly."

"Did you meet one last night?"

"Not exactly."

"I'm assuming since you called and sound cheery that the sheriff arrived in the 'nick of time' as they say in the old westerns, and you're safe and sound."

"I am. Thank you. I never know if these phones are working or not."

"I picked up bits and pieces of the conversation, but the Buddy Danko and X-Ray part were real clear."

"Thanks. Have you found Dee yet?"

"Nope. There's no message on our machine. She has my

cell phone. No call. I checked with the house where she stayed; no word there."

"Have you checked the hospitals and morgue in San Diego yet? Maybe she got hurt and didn't have any ID on her."

"I returned home late last night to a rush assignment to find and serve a witness in the Johnson case. I'm working on that now."

"I'm thinking of coming home to help you with Dee. The sheriff has agreed to drop by the Texas Rangers' lab later today and give a DNA sample. I'm not sure if that's going to be good enough to check against the spleen, but it'll get things going here."

"I'm worried about Dee."

"So am I."

"What if Henry Lee has hurt Dee?"

"Then he'll have me and the entire city of Zavalla to deal with. They really love her here."

Chapter Nineteen

Slim hadn't finished fishing yet, but Marshall family members had towed the rental unit to his garage. Gina offered to drive Mel to the airport in Beaumont.

Mel and Gina ate a hearty Texas breakfast at Tiny Opal's Café. Mel took scraps to Slick, who sat patiently in the truck's front seat. Bobby Gene's four-wheeler rolled across the parking lot, and small pieces of gravel and dust spewed through the air.

"Where you-all going so early this morning?" Bobby Gene asked.

"Gina's running me to Beaumont. I've got a connecting flight to Houston, then into San Diego."

"No word from Dee, huh?"

"Not one."

"That's not like her, disappearing and all. Except when she's hiding from Henry Lee."

"That's what I'm concerned about."

"Should I go with you?" Bobby Gene asked.

"No, but thank you. I think between Johnnie and me and

the police departments up and down the Southern California coast — we'll find her."

At the airport, Mel hugged Gina. "Thank you so much for all your help."

"Aw, you're welcome. Did you take the gun with you?"

"No. I duct taped it to the underside of the chest in the cabin."

"So, you're coming back?"

"Probably. Got to find Dee first.

By mid-afternoon, Mel's plane landed in San Diego. She stopped by the same rental company and left with a new car. One, they promised her was brand new, with few miles, and in excellent condition.

She dropped by the San Diego Police Department and called X-Ray from their parking lot.

"Glad to hear you're in one piece," X-Ray said.

"You heard about my drop-in, huh?" Mel asked.

"Johnnie called."

"Did you pick up a photo of Dee?"

"Yep, but just faxed it over there. Ask for Detective Rhonda Wilder. She's got it."

"Any news in Orange or LA County?"

"No Jane Doe at the coroner here. We're checking the local hospitals, nothing yet."

"I'll check back with you when I'm finished here."

"Fine. Good luck."

With that final click, Mel had walked into the lobby and asked the front desk for the detective. She paced the length of the tiny corridor when she heard the clicking of heels approaching. She turned to see the most beautiful redhead smiling, her right hand extended. They shook hands.

"Good afternoon, Detective Wilder. X-Ray said you were expecting me."

"Hi, Mel. The fax came in a few moments ago."

"Did you question the tech at the medical lab yet?"

"I spoke with her yesterday. She said the woman was there one minute, then changed her mind about the test and like almost ran out of the building."

"What was her state of mind?"

"Agitated. But not crying or anything like that."

"She didn't follow her or see where she went?"

"Nope. She had a line of patients waiting for their tests."

"She didn't hear or see anything unusual after that?"

Rhonda shook her head. "Nope. She stayed in her spot until long after your associate left. So, he'd have a better idea how to find her than the tech. Sorry."

"Me too. Do you have any DBs you can't ID?"

"Let's drop by the coroner's office. It's just across the street."

Wilder stood head-to-head and kept pace with Mel, as they crossed with the light and chatted about the perfect weather.

"How long you been with the San Diego Police Department?" Mel asked.

"Long enough to be cynical."

"One shift, huh?" Mel responded.

They both laughed.

"Are all morgue's this sterile white?" Mel asked.

"I don't know. I do know the smell stays the same."

"You got that."

Inside, Wilder motioned to the receptionist, and the double-wide metal doors clicked open. Mel and Wilder walked down a tiled hallway to a small office. Wilder leaned in one open door, "Doc, you here?"

"Come on in. What can I do for you today?"

They slipped into the already cramped office filled knee-high with medical journals, papers, charts, and photos.

"This is an investigator from Orange County, Mel Walker. She's looking for a DB — a Jane Doe."

Mel extended her hand. "Good afternoon, Doc."

"Got a picture?" He asked.

Wilder handed him the copy. The doctor lifted his half-glasses to his almost-bald forehead, squinted, and studied it for a few seconds.

"Mmm." He paused. "I got a gal here, but this doesn't look much like her." He looked at Mel and motioned. "Come on. Want to take a look?"

"Sure."

"Seen a dead body before?" Wilder asked.

"Sure. My Dad was a cop," Mel replied.

"Was?" Wilder asked.

"Somebody murdered him."

"I hate that," the doctor responded.

He walked to the row of chrome drawers stacked three-high, glanced at a flip-chart hanging from one of them, then jerked that drawer open. Inside, the shrouded body lay on a shiny chrome slab. The doctor pulled back the sheet as far as the shoulder area. Mel looked at the body and swallowed hard.

She sighed. "No. That's not her."

"Too bad," the doctor said, as he recovered the cadaver and pushed the drawer shut.

"No. That's not bad. I want this lady alive. She hired me to look for her missing child."

Rhonda spoke first. "Did you hear about the FBI sting? They found a lot of small children near Chula Vista."

"My associate, Johnnie Blake, came down here and he and my missing mother looked through the group. But the female child wasn't there."

"Now that's too bad," the doctor said.

"I agree there. I need to find them both and in a hurry. The estranged husband might be tied up with their disappearance," Mel said.

"While I'm here, I gotta question for you, Doc," Mel said.

"Sure."

"Can you take DNA from a spleen that might be that of a niece to DNA from the niece's uncle on the mother's side?"

"The short answer is 'Yes,'" Doc said. "It's medically complicated, but you can." He nodded.

Rhonda and the doctor said their thanks and goodbyes, and Mel made a run at all the local hospitals, Dee's photo in hand. No luck.

After leaving the last hospital in Chula Vista, Mel stopped at a light near Interstate 5 waiting her turn to go north, then swerved out of that lane, and took the south on-ramp instead.

I'm very near the border. I might as well check, she thought.

With San Diego twenty miles behind her, Mel turned on the radio and daydreamed in light traffic. As American civilization dwindled, a wasteland came into view. Barren hills rolled to the north, grassy marshes to the south, at the U.S. border with Mexico at Tijuana. She thought of the conundrum where the richest nation collided with one of the poorest. In her wandering thoughts, she almost missed the huge sign LAST EXIT IN U.S.A. She swerved toward the off-ramp, followed the signs, and located a parking space in the already crowded lot near the Immigration and Naturalization office.

An imposing metal barricade fence more than twenty-feet

tall appeared impenetrable along both sides of the border. Mel waited on the curb and allowed traffic to pass. She quickly realized it wasn't the Berlin Wall, as small groups of Hispanics toting small cloth bundles managed to slip through the fence to freedom on the American side and scatter to avoid capture.

A quiet sense of despair filled the dusty air and mingled with smells of oil and gas fumes from cars and trucks lined like metal chains across eighteen lanes of traffic. Lines of anxious walking travelers carrying their purchases wound out of view on the Mexico side. As they approached the border, they waited, then shuffled slowly down the sandy street, into the building, through the turnstile, and down the long narrow aisle to America. Drug-sniffing dogs on short leads paused and circled and sniffed each returning person and their packages. One slowed Mel's progress.

She asked his handler, "I'm an investigator from Orange County looking for a missing person. Who can I see?"

"Our inspector on duty is in that office." He pointed to a small unmarked white door.

She knocked.

The officer dressed in a green uniform opened the door.

"Hi. I'm Mel Walker, an investigator from Orange County." She handed him her business card.

"What can I do for you?" He asked as he motioned her inside.

"I don't know if you can help me or not. I'm looking for a missing woman. Here's her photo."

He chuckled slightly and shook his head. He looked at Dee's picture. "I don't know what you expect, Miss ah..." he glanced at her card, "Miss Walker."

"I know it's a long shot," she said.

"It's more than a long shot. How long's she been missing?"

"Mmm, three days."

"Well, Miss Walker, we're open 24/7, and in that length of time we've seen almost 90,000 pedestrians cross the border back into the United States."

"Thirty thousand people a day?" She gulped.

"And three to five times that many on holidays and weekends."

"Jeez, I had no idea."

"I could do this for you. There are law enforcement agencies that come to us with bulletins we call 'lookouts.'"

"Like smugglers, people with priors, FBI's most wanted?"

"Yeah, like that. Missing kids, too. Let me have a copy, and when each shift musters, we'll see it's posted at each station. If she happens to come through — if she hasn't already — we'll see her."

"Do you tape people's faces as they walk through?"

"You mean like video you'd find in a convenience store?"

"Yeah."

"Yes, we do. But you'd have to get a court order, and the amount of tape you'd have to scan would not seem to be the best use of your time. However, that's just my opinion."

"I agree. Anyway, I don't know if she even crossed the border. It was just a hunch. I was in the area and thought I'd try."

"Let me make a copy of the photo and staple your business card to it. That's about all I can do for now. You know, if she drove through instead of walking, we're talking about 30,000 million cars a year."

"Your port of entry jobs must be like trying to cure cancer with a bandage and some ointment."

He sighed, "That's about it."

Mel drove the rental unit north on Interstate 5. Each lane was filled with rushing and rage-filled travelers trying to pass miles of eighteen wheelers. Interstate 5 became Highway 405; this juncture is known as one of the heaviest traveled areas in the entire United States. That's when the rental car sputtered and died. Right in the middle of an eight-lane highway in rush-hour traffic.

Chapter Twenty

"They're going to quit renting cars to you if you keep break-ing them," Johnnie said, as he arrived to pick up Mel off the freeway.

"They weren't too happy, but neither am I."

Johnnie grabbed her luggage from the trunk and placed it in the Mustang. "I can't believe I beat the tow-truck here."

"What else is new? Look at this traffic."

Mel's stalled situation had cars in both the northbound and southbound lanes in a stop-and-go mode. Horns honked, and people cussed at her when they realized her dilemma.

She hollered back at one guy. "So, what's your problem?"

Johnnie patted her arm. "Now, don't get huffy. Some people in these cars have guns, and right now you don't."

Red light-bars spun as the tow truck lumbered toward her in the emergency lane. He stopped traffic even more as he maneuvered in front and backed up.

"I have Triple A," was Mel's greeting.

"That's good," the guy replied, as he grabbed the chains and lay on the concrete to hook up the disabled vehicle.

A California Highway Patrol vehicle raced to the scene, and that only added a sense of curiosity and more slow-down.

"Good grief," Mel said when she spotted the black-and-white. "What else could happen?"

"We could find Dee." Johnnie said.

"That'd be great."

"Well, maybe we did."

"What?"

"There's a Jane Doe at Harbor View. X-Ray is there now with a photo. He's waiting on us."

Chapter Twenty-One

They sped to the hospital near Harbour Pointe and parked near the emergency entrance. The whooshing sound of electronic doors greeted them. A uniformed officer posted in the ER recognized Mel and approached.

"Detective Ramirez is in ICU. Said to tell you to join him."

"I hate this place," Mel said, as she and Johnnie traversed the shiny corridors to the Intensive Care Unit. A nurse met them at the entrance.

"Me too." He rubbed his arm. "The cops are right. I can tell the weather from my wound."

"We're here to see Detective Ramirez. I'm Mel Walker. This is Johnnie Blake."

The nurse motioned for them to follow her through the double doors marked NO ENTRY, past the curtained alcoves filled with patients, to a small glassed-in corner room. There, surrounded by tubing, needles, trays, and technology monitoring her every breath, lay Dee.

"It's her, isn't it?" X-Ray asked.

"Yep." Johnnie walked to one side of the bed and replied.

Mel moved to the opposite side of the bed and grasped Dee's hand. "She looks like hell. What happened to her?"

"We don't know for sure. She's heavily bruised, couple of broken ribs, some internal damage, probably some brain damage."

"Was she beaten?" Johnnie asked.

"Could have been," X-Ray said.

"Could it have been a car accident?" Johnnie asked.

"Anything's possible," X-Ray said.

"Are you running a rape kit?" Mel asked.

"Sure," X-Ray said.

"Dee, Dee," Mel called to her.

"She's unconscious. They ran a CAT scan and are waiting on the report right now," X-Ray said.

A young nurse entered the room. "Can you give us information on this Jane Doe? We need to notify the next of kin."

"Her family lives in Texas. I just flew in from there. I'll write down the information for you. On second thought, she lived in a battered woman shelter in Long Beach. Maybe you should contact them first. She may not want to be found."

They listened to the labored sounds of the respirator breathing in and out for Dee, the beeps from the heart monitor, and studied her injuries for a minute. X-Ray spoke first.

"From the moment you picked her up, Johnnie, what happened?"

"She was waiting at the curb in front of the shelter when I arrived."

"What time was that?" X-Ray asked as he took notes.

"About 7:35 a.m.," Johnnie said. "She was wearing a blue-and-white checked gingham jumper-type dress with big pockets. She wore a white blouse with little lace trim around the arms and collar under that. Sandals. No jewelry. Hair in a ponytail at the nape of her neck. Blue bow I think. She carried no purse and nothing in her hands."

"Did you stop along the way?"

"I had gassed up the night before. But we stopped around Dana Point for a bite of breakfast."

"Anything unusual there?"

"No."

"Was she out of your sight for even one minute?" Mel asked.

"No."

"Were you followed?" X-Ray asked.

"I didn't think so. I can't be sure, but anything is possible I guess."

X-Ray asked, "What happened when you got to that center where the children were?"

"She was getting very nervous by that time. Wringing her hands. I gave her a tissue from the console. We walked in, spoke with the attendant, looked at dozens of photos, and interviewed with the FBI agent in charge. He then walked through a large room where the children played with some toys. But Angel wasn't there."

"What was Dee's reaction to that?" Mel asked.

"She cried. She gripped my hand and cried."

"Was she out of your sight there?" Mel asked.

"No. We left my card with them, along with Angel's photo in case anyone else was found, and we drove over to the lab. Once there, Dee put her name on the reception chart, picked up a newspaper, and sat next to me. The waiting room was filled with people, and more came in while we waited. About five minutes later I had to go to the restroom. I asked where it was, and told Dee I'd be right back. That's the last time I saw her."

"She didn't ask any questions? You didn't talk? Anything?" Mel asked.

"I know we're scraping the bottom of the barrel for ideas here, but she gave me no hint whatsoever that she wouldn't allow someone to swab the inside of her mouth."

X-Ray asked Mel, "Is there any chance Angel isn't her child? Maybe that's why she refused the DNA test?"

"That was my first thought too. But her brother, the sheriff there in Zavalla, told me he saw her quote pregnant as a cow with Angel unquote."

"Well, let's think this out further," X-Ray said.

"Assuming Dee is the mother, maybe Angel isn't Henry's baby, and she's afraid her infidelity will be revealed," Mel said.

"Maybe that's why Henry Lee beat Dee. He thought Angel wasn't his child," Johnnie said.

"Or knew for certain?" X-Ray said.

Chapter Twenty-Two

X-Ray obtained a court order for the unconscious Dee's DNA. Mel received a fax from Sheriff Paul Ames Marshall who assured her he had talked with the coroner, and his DNA could be identified with that of the organ. He had his test done, and they were waiting for the results. The sheriff wanted to know if there was any news on Dee. Mel lied.

Johnnie and Mel and sat in the reception area of Walker Investigations' office and drank coffee.

"Why'd you lie to the sheriff?"

"Johnnie, I can count on one hand the number of people I can truly trust."

Mel sorted through several stacks of mail and opened those that appeared to be personal.

"Where are the bills?"

"I paid them while you were gone."

"Thanks. How are we doing?"

"Financially or business-wise?"

"Both."

"We're solvent thanks in part to the county paying us for

the Ramirez case. I have several cases with multiple defendants and lots of witness work-ups that will keep us busy until the year end. Assuming you can help someday."

She raised her eyebrows. "Excuse me. You got me in this non-paying gig with Dee and Angel."

"Correction. Rosa started this."

"Speaking of Rosa, I'm hungry. Think dinner's ready."

"Your first night home? Of course, dinner's ready. I'm betting it's her specialty, enchiladas."

The smell of cumin and mole sauce hit Mel's nostrils the minute she opened the front door. "I'm home," she called out.

"Correction, we're home," Johnnie added.

Rosa shuffled to the front door with hugs all around. Her spatula dripped with cheese that she wiped on her apron. "Madre Mia, I've been missing you so much. I'm so glad you're home. I can't believe I got you in this mess."

"Don't fuss over me."

"If I don't, then who can?" Rosa asked.

"I can't believe I let you get me involved either." Mel licked another drip of cheese. "But you could make it up to me by having my favorite Mexican dish tonight."

"I got it," Rosa smiled. Her white teeth gleamed against her brown skin. She returned to the kitchen and called out over her back. "X-Ray going to join us. He's hungry too. He has news for you."

While Johnnie unloaded Mel's luggage, she showered and changed clothes and reached the upstairs landing when the doorbell rang.

"I'll get it," Johnnie's lilting voice caused Mel to smile.

"Come in. Dinner's almost ready." He raised his voice and lowered his octave, "Mel, X-Ray's here."

Rosa cleaned up the kitchen and left the trio drinking fresh coffee on the patio. They watched the bright sun become an orange-sherbet sunset. It hung suspended for a breath, then quickly dropped off the edge of the earth, or so it seemed. They sat in silence.

"How's Dee?" Mel spoke first.

"Doc Townsend said most of her wounds are superficial, lots of bruising and small cuts. She has several fractured ribs. But something happened to her head. She's suffered a major head trauma," X-Ray said.

"Got an idea what happened to her?" Johnnie asked.

"Could be a beating...."

Mel interrupted, "Could it have been injuries from a car accident?"

X-Ray nodded, "Could."

"Does Doc have any idea how long she'll be unconscious?" Mel asked.

"No way of telling. Her brain waves are strong, so she isn't like — brain dead or anything that appears severe."

"So, it isn't really life-threatening?" Johnnie asked.

"I hope to know more tomorrow. I asked Barry to stop by and give her a look."

"I thought you said she wasn't going to die?" Johnnie asked.

"Who better than our very own coroner for a forensic exam?"

Chapter Twenty-Three

Mel and Johnnie arrived at the hospital early the following morning. They waited in the hallway while the Orange County Coroner's crime lab technicians took fingernail clippings, matter from under Dee's nails, combed her hair for particles, and photographed the injured parts of her body.

Barry Zabel, the coroner, stepped into the hall and snapped off his rubber gloves. "Good morning guys. We meet again."

"Except you have a live one this time," Johnnie said.

"I must admit when X-Ray called I was surprised. This is very unusual for me. But, I may get her yet." Barry ran his hand through his soft black-gray hair and yawned.

"I hope you're wrong. You have some thoughts?" Mel asked.

X-Ray exited a nearby lounge and motioned for the trio to join him.

"I hope you're right, but the CAT scan agrees with me. Yes, I do have some ideas as a matter of fact," Barry said.

They turned off the sound on the television and pulled chairs in a semi-circle around Barry. Now alone in the waiting room, they closed the door to visitors.

"Okay, let's have it," X-Ray said.

"Well, the scrape marks on her arms and legs are concrete burns like those you'd get skateboarding or in-line skating."

"Like when you fall?" Johnnie asked.

"Or being dragged maybe by a moving vehicle."

"The CAT scan indicates a major closed head wound. There are several possibilities...."

"That we're not going to like?" Johnnie asked.

"Right. Worst case scenario, she'll die. Or worse than that, she'll live in a vegetative state until some ripe old age."

"Oh, my God," Mel whispered, as she stared into space.

"Can surgery change her condition?" Johnnie asked.

Barry responded, "The best neurosurgeon in Orange County has been assigned to look at her tests. We'll know more later. But my professional opinion is she's a candidate for my office sooner than normally expected."

"Damn, I hate that," X-Ray added.

"We'll get those bastards." Johnnie looked at X-Ray, then at Mel. "We will, won't we?"

Mel patted his arm, "I'm damn sure going to try."

"In the meantime, the specialists are doing what they can, and I'll do the lab work and get you some reports as quickly as I can." Barry stood and shook hands with everyone and left.

"Did Dee ever talk about anyone else in her life beside Henry, who may have a reason to harm her?" X-Ray asked.

Johnnie said, "We talked on the way down the coast about her life a bit. She told me she'd dated several guys briefly, but wasn't interested. One guy kinda bugged her, but she didn't appear concerned about him. "

"More to the point, was anyone interested in her?" Mel asked.

"Yeah, that guy who bugged her. Him. They met at an AA meeting."

"Oh, right, another great place to look for the future father of your children." Mel asked, "What was his name?"

"That I did forget."

X-Ray said, "How will we get it? AA is anonymous."

"And only first names."

"So, I join her chapter of AA."

"I've been meaning to speak with you about that." Mel jostled Johnnie with her elbow and smiled.

X-Ray interrupted their banter, "You both should attend. Maybe Mel can draw out this guy if you develop a name. Then I'll run him through the system and eliminate him as a suspect."

"In the meantime, Angel is still missing."

"Don't forget Angel."

"I never will."

Chapter Twenty-Four

Johnnie stood in the steaming heat on the battered women's shelter front porch and pleaded, "I know you must respect the anonymity, but I can't ask Dee right now what AA group she belongs to." He smiled and cupped his hands together.

The woman stood behind the locked door and squinted through the screen door. She took a drag on her cigarette and inhaled deep and long. Smoke expelled through her pores as she responded, "Why do you want to know about group?"

"I need to see if anyone who attends knows anyone who might want to hurt her."

"You mean besides Henry Lee?"

"Yeah."

"Okay, but you didn't hear this from me."

"I agree," Johnnie said.

"You know that little church on Fourth Street near the park?"

"Next door to the coffee place that does poetry readings?"

"That one."

"Yeah."

"AA meets at that church on Tuesday nights. Seven-thirty I think."

"I really appreciate it."

"Knock yourself out." The woman slammed the door shut, but waifs of smoke cleared the screen invading Johnnie's space.

He coughed all the way to the car.

"Mel, Sheriff Marshall here. X-Ray called me. Why didn't you tell me you found Dee?"

"I could lie and say 'I thought it was X-Ray's job to call you.' In reality, I'm not sure who to trust."

"You can trust me. Trust me. How's Dee?"

"She's still unconscious, but her brain waves are strong."

"She's gonna die, isn't she?"

"Only God knows that for sure, Sheriff. One thing I do know, they've got the best specialists working with her."

"Who's gonna pay for all that?"

"No one at the hospital talked with me about that. She's probably on welfare. I can't honestly say."

"I called with some news, but mostly bad."

"The DNA test?"

He sighed. "Yeah. Me and the spleen – we're a match."

"Now, don't get yourself down. We can all live without a spleen."

"I know that. But..."

"Listen, Sheriff, the cop in you is working overtime. Remember my daddy was a detective for many years. I know how your brain works."

"Angel was my baby, too."

"We'll get her back. I'm not giving up on this case."

"You got any ideas?"

Johnnie entered Mel's office, waved, motioned for a cup of

coffee, and walked to the kitchen.

"Johnnie and I are following some leads from here."

"If I can help, just let me know."

"I will. Bye."

Mel joined Johnnie and stirred a spoonful of sugar into her cup, as she leaned against the counter.

"And we know what?" Johnnie asked.

"The DNA is a match."

"Shit, I hate that."

"Me too. Did you get anything in Long Beach?"

"Yeah, a woman at the shelter told me where the AA meetings are held. It's tonight. Care to join me?"

"Hi, my name is Bill, and I'm an alcoholic."

Everyone collectively replied, "Hi Bill."

Bill told the story of his addiction, but Mel blocked out most of it while she focused on members of the mixed audience. Men and women in various shapes and sizes, from multiple ethnicities and ages from the early twenties to late seventies, filled the small chapel. While Bill spoke, they shuffled their feet and scooted the white portable chairs into a better viewing place.

The air stung with a mixture of stale tobacco, aging colognes, and body odors. One Mel recognized.

"Mary Jane," Mel whispered to Johnnie.

He sniffed the air, smiled, and nodded. He turned toward a young man in the row ahead of them and pointed.

After several people shared their experiences, Mel spoke. "Hi, my name is Mel, and I drink too often and too much."

"Hello Mel," the group chorused. Several chuckled.

"I know this may be poor judgment on my part, but my sharing tonight concerns a woman named Dee Dee who lies in Harbour Pointe Hospital in a deep coma tonight. Her child, Angel," she purposely paused, "is missing. I've been asked by the family in Texas to find Angel. I'm trying to find out what happened to Dee Dee, and why she may die. I believe she attended this meeting and if any of you know anything that might help me, I'm going to leave a couple of my cards here. Please call me. I will not involve you in any way. I will maintain your anonymity."

One woman, who stared at the floor, wept and knotted a tissue through her gnarled fingers. Several men shifted their weight and changed their open body language to one of crossed arms and legs. Some looked at the floor. Others looked at no particular point on the ceiling. The uncomfortable silence was broken when one of the group men, slapped his knees and stood.

"With that cherry and disruptive note from an intruder, why don't we take a brief coffee, cigarette, donut, potty break and give her a chance to kindly leave?"

Everyone stood and gathered in tight pairs and groups and chatted like old friends. They all ignored Mel and Johnnie. She whispered to Johnnie, "I feel like a pearl seed outside the oyster."

He shrugged like he didn't know who she was talking to or about, and he joined one of the pairs that widened their circle to admit him. She caught the subtly of the hint, dropped some cards on the chair, and walked out to her car alone.

Mel saved the last of her work, yawned and shut off the computer when she heard a car enter the driveway. She recognized the Pumpkin's muffler and stepped out into the backyard to greet him.

"What are you doing at the office this late?" Johnnie asked.

"Waiting on you. I knew you had to come home sooner or later."

"Boy, what they don't do with alcohol, they do with coffee. I'm going to be awake all night."

"Got the jitters, huh?"

"And how."

"Was it worth it?"

"You bet." Johnnie parked the Mustang in his garage, pulled down the door, and locked it; then walked with Mel toward their office kitchen.

He pulled out a note pad and flipped back a few pages. "Remember the woman who cried?"

"Older woman, mid-fifties, gray hair, stooped shoulders, plain print dress, pink and white as I recall, flip-flops?"

"That one, yeah."

"Name's Peggy. She was Angel's babysitter and lives at the shelter."

"She must be devastated."

"She feels very responsible for not saving Angel from her abductor."

"What's her story?"

"By the way, she isn't fifty something. She's thirty-six."

Mel poured her and John a glass of water and joined him at the kitchen table. "Ouch."

"Tough life. Anyway, Peggy works as a waitress at one of the dives near Terminal Island. She's been there for twelve years in the same place, so she knows everyone, and they know her. Dee and Henry Lee's been drinking there since they moved from Texas. Both came separately when they broke up. Dee and Henry Lee had lots of knockdown, drag-outs, and he was eighty-sixth a bunch of times. Peggy said Henry Lee was meaner and stronger than their bouncer who eventually gave up trying to negotiate with him or toss him out."

"Why didn't Dee just stay home with Angel or go somewhere else to drink?"

"You're asking me?"

Mel shrugged, "Did she have any ideas?"

"She said she and her daughter arrived early and waited outside Angel's class that day, and Angel just didn't appear. She spoke with Angel's teacher, but between them, they didn't see any stranger, and Peggy didn't see Henry Lee."

"She got there before class let out?"

"Yeah."

"I guess Angel could have left out another exit."

"Dee had told Angel that Peggy would pick her up after school and knew which exit to wait on her."

"And Angel hadn't missed school that day. We checked that already."

"I didn't. Did you?"

"Yeah, Johnnie. She attended every class. Did Peggy know of anyone else who expressed a romantic interest in Dee?"

"Several of the guys from the bar flirted from time to time, but Dee didn't reciprocate. Peggy did have an idea of someone she liked better than Henry Lee as the kidnapper."

"Who?"

"The guy from AA who was toking." Johnnie flipped back and forth between the pages in his notepad. "It was eerie. This guy walks up to the group and reeks of marijuana. He's spaced. I was getting a contact high from the fumes. Several people chuckled, and when he spoke with me, they backed away and regrouped in another area."

"Is it someone we've screened before?"

"No. First time his name's come up. I called X-Ray and left a message to check him out. His name is Greg Montgomery and get this. I offered him a ride home because he recently had an accident with his car, and it's in the shop."

"And you have the shop's name?"

"Is the Pope Polish?"

"And you gave that info to X-Ray too?"

"Mel, knowing you as I do, would I do that?"

"Good man. I don't want to destroy evidence or leave ours either, but the night's young...."

"Ours? Oh Lord, I'm on a contact high, got the jitters, and now we're going to jail."

Chapter Twenty-Five

Mel and Johnnie dressed in Ninja black from head to foot, took medical gloves and paper feet coverings, and grabbed the long-handled bolt cutters from the garage.

"Mel, I have a better idea. Let's wait until morning, park out front, and knock on the door. Like regular folk. In the daytime. Just put our card on the owner and say, 'Hey, we're investigators. Can we look at Greg's car?'"

"That wouldn't be near as much fun."

"But oh, so much more safe."

They passed the body shop twice to make sure they had the right address. A small frame building set on the back side of the property away from the road. A seven-foot tall chain link fence surrounded the area. The dark night and no perimeter lighting shielded them from being easily noticed.

"Look," Mel said, as she parked nearby. "They have that barbed wire that prisons use to keep people in."

"That's a good message, Mel. It's probably electrified too."

"Or they could have a night watchman. Better yet a junk-yard dog."

"Oh, I wish you hadn't said that."

Johnnie put on gloves, grabbed the foot coverings, a flashlight, and exited the car. Mel followed him, picked up a couple of pebbles nearby, and threw them at the fence.

"See? No sizzle."

"That's the good news," Johnnie said. He shined the light near a large metal sign that hung by one steel loop near the gate. While bent, weather-beaten, and filled with holes from years of BB pellets, the sign's message appeared clear to Johnnie. "Here's the other news."

The unmistakable warning carried the silhouette of a Doberman that stood at attention over the words, "I can make it to the fence in twenty seconds. Can you?"

"That's real clear. I can't run that fast," Johnnie said.

"Silly. That's an old sign," Mel said, as she dismissed him.

"So, now he's an old Doberman who can make it to the fence in forty seconds. He still has me beat. Wish we had some food for him."

"Check the fence line around to the back and see if there's a gate or other opening we might use rather than cut the fence. I've got some doggy cookies in my trunk."

"I should have known that," Johnnie said. He shook his head and paced the front area, then disappeared out of sight down an alley.

They both met at the end of the alley a few minutes later for Johnnie's report. "Okay, there's a dumpster area with access through a small gate into the yard. Did you hear any barking?"

"No, and I would certainly think with this activity he'd be eating us alive by now."

"Or he's a heavy sleeper."

Mel laughed. "You are too funny. Let's go."

"Last time I went into a dark alley with you, I got shot."

They walked the rear fence line and found a small gate that wasn't locked. "Is it breaking and entering when it isn't locked?" Johnnie asked.

"You don't want to know," Mel replied. "What kind of car does he have?"

"It's a blue Mazda, four-door. Should have damage to the right rear fender and bumper."

"What did he say happened?"

"Said someone must have side-swiped him while it was parked in a shopping center."

The area remained quiet as Mel and Johnnie checked the twenty some-odd cars in the lot.

"Here it is," Johnnie whispered. "Not repaired yet. That's good."

"Is there any visible blood on the bumper or fender?"

"None that I can see. Now if X-Ray's crime scene unit was here, they would have those special lights and swabs and good stuff they use to detect all that important evidence – legally."

"Let's check inside the car." Mel opened the front passenger door; and Johnnie shined the light to the floor, seat, and dash areas. "Oh, look at that." Mel pointed to drops near the headrest.

"That looks like blood."

Mel stood straight and looked around. "Okay, I'm done here," she whispered, as the hair stood on the back of her neck.

"What's the matter? Do we call X-Ray and tell him about Greg's car?"

"Only if we can get to the gate alive in forty seconds," Mel hollered, as she tossed a handful of cookies from her pocket and ran to the exit with Johnnie fast on her heels.

Chapter Twenty-Six

"That was the biggest blackest dog I ever saw," Mel laughed so hard, she held her sides.

"Why didn't he stop us long before he did?"

"Maybe he was deaf."

"He scared me; he was very fast. I'm gonna have to change my pants."

Mel and Johnnie laughed all the way home.

"Good morning, X-Ray," Mel said.

"You sure are cheery. It's awful early in the morning for you to be in trouble," X-Ray said.

"No. Nothing like that. Johnnie learned more information from that Greg Montgomery guy that we thought you should have."

She described the car and the damage as told to Johnnie and suggested his CSU check it out, especially for Dee's DNA.

"Did you find any blood?" X-Ray calmly asked.

"Ye...you might look for some. I would have no way of knowing that."

"Right."

Mel changed the subject, "Any word on Dee's condition?"

"I haven't checked the hospital yet, but I'll keep you in the loop."

"Good."

"Talk with you later, when we check out that blood you didn't already find."

"Whatever are you talking about?"

Mel had washed their black outfits, answered a mound of phone messages, and paid some bills when the phone rang.

"Hi, honey."

"Lucas. You sound so far away. You always sound far away."

"I'm in Liberia today."

"Is that Africa?"

"Yes."

"I miss you."

"I was so looking forward to spending some time with you in Texas. Sorry, we got our wires crossed. Is that case closed?"

"No, regrettably it isn't. We haven't found the little girl who's missing, and now her mother has been injured and is in grave condition."

"That's terrible. So, you'll be going back to Houston?"

"Yeah, but I don't know when. We have a few leads and, as the days pass without any new leads, finding her alive isn't promising right now."

"Listen, honey, I'm on my cell and not sure how long we have to speak. Maybe I can get this wrapped up in a few days, and you could fly back to Houston. Maybe I could fly out and join you for a few days. Whatever. Would love to love you."

"I'm flexible, and I'd love that too. Let me see how things are here, and I'll call you."

"Fine. Honey, you're breaking up."

"Can you hear me?" Mel asked.

"I can't hear you, honey. Gotta run. Later love."

High winds from an offshore disturbance blew six to eight-foot waves crashing along the shore behind Mel's home. Her hat flew off several times during her morning run, and she finally crushed the cloth cap into her back pocket. She passed several dogs and their masters who chased sticks, balls, or other treasures. One large golden retriever brushed past her on his way to victory, knocking her off-balance, and she fell. A man running slightly behind her came to her rescue.

"Are you all right?" He asked.

"Yes, thank you," Mel said.

"Jake is a friendly guy. He's just dedicated to his job."

"I can see that." She brushed her hair away from her face and dusted the sand off her clothes.

The middle-aged man with gray curly hair smiled. He wiped off his glasses and said, "This isn't a pick-up line, but don't you live around here?"

"Yes, just on the knoll above there." She pointed.

"I thought I'd seen you run before."

They began to walk, and Jake bounced back to his master and returned the green rubber alligator to his feet.

The man picked it up and tossed it again, this time behind them and Jake lumbered away, his shiny golden-red coat fluttering in the wind.

"I run when I can. I work, and I'm not home that often."

"What do you do?"

"I'm a PI."

"No, shit!"

"No, shit," she replied. "And you?"

As the man answered, "I'm a lawyer," her pocket vibrated.

"I married one once. Excuse me," she turned away from the noisy surf. "Hello. This is Mel...Hi, Johnnie....uh uh. Great. I'll be there in thirty minutes. Don't let him get away. I'm on the beach with a lawyer and a dog. No, not Taylor." She laughed. "No Johnnie. The lawyer is not a dog. He has a dog. It's two different things." She flipped the top down and slipped the phone into her jean's pocket. "Sorry about that."

"On the job, huh?"

"Always."

"Don't think much of lawyers, huh?"

"I try not to think about them at all. I really have to run. Nice to meet you."

"But you didn't meet me. My name is...."

His name was lost in the crashing surf and the widening distance Mel made as she waved goodbye over her shoulder. She jogged the distance to the wooden stairs, took two at a time up to the concrete walkway behind the ocean-view homes, then sprinted to her back door. She never looked back.

Mel drove the traffic-challenged Pacific Coast Highway toward Harbour View Hospital and impatiently tapped her fingers on the steering wheel. Over the sounds of Dave Koz, her phone rang.

"Hello. Mel speaking."

"Hi. I've been thinking what to do."

"What Johnnie?"

"Greg's still in there with Dee, just patting her hand and talking to her."

"Has her condition changed?"

"Nope."

"Don't let him get away. What are you thinking?"

"We probably should wait until he leaves the hospital and

trail him. Let's not confront him here."

"What if the police also have an informant at the hospital, and they've already called X-Ray?"

"I hadn't thought of that."

"One thing for sure, don't let the police talk with him until you and I do."

"Uh-oh. I think he's getting up."

"Stop him outside. Offer to take him somewhere for lunch." Mel suggested.

"Where? We can't go to Bernie's."

"Why not. A cop hangout is the perfect place. So long as he doesn't have any marijuana on him. I'll meet you there."

"What if X-Ray has a photo of his driver's license? They'll surely recognize him if they come in."

"I'll call X-Ray and divert him. The worst that could happen is we'll all interview him together."

"I don't think Chief Murdoch will let you do that again."

"You underestimate my charm."

"Right. Is that how you lost your gun permit?"

"Smart-aleck. I'm almost at Bernie's. See you soon."

She called the police department, but X-Ray was out, and she left a bogus phone message for him. She pulled into the graveled lot behind Bernie's to find five Highway Patrol cars and three local undercover cop cars parked there.

She pushed the screen door open. The hinges that badly needed oil squeaked, announcing her appearance.

"Hi Cookie," Mel said. "I need a booth."

A male voice replied to Cookie. "I got one right here for you."

Chapter Twenty-Seven

"How could you possibly believe I wouldn't know everything that goes on near a crime victim in a hospital?" X-Ray asked, as he patted the booth seat and encouraged Mel to join him.

"I could dream," Mel replied, as she slid in beside him.

"Dream on. Is Johnnie bringing him here?"

"Yeah."

Cookie approached the table, withdrew a pencil from deep within one of the large red curls piled on the top of her head, and snatched the order pad from her dingy apron. "Hey, Mel. How're you doing? Our lunch special is meatloaf."

"I'm fine. I think I'll take a tuna sandwich today, wheat toast, and fruit. Hold the fries. And a diet anything." Mel added, "We have two more joining us, but I think we should order now."

X-Ray nodded and gave Cookie his order as well.

"Are you mad?" Mel asked after Cookie left.

"Disappointed, but not surprised. I don't know why you think you can circumvent the police department on matters like this and not get in trouble."

"Am I in trouble?"

"I hope not."

"Is it too much to ask how the DNA tests are coming on the blood from the car's headrest?"

X-Ray gave her his most outraged cop-look. "How did you know it was the headrest?" His tone filled the room, and several cops turned to see if everything was okay.

She smelled anger as only X-Ray could exude. She had a ready answer. "Because Dee has a head injury. Where else in the car would be the blood be?"

"You're good. Quick and really good."

Cookie returned with their drinks.

"Thank you," Mel quietly replied, as she sipped her cola.

A few minutes later the back door opened and in walked Johnnie. When Johnnie spotted Mel sitting with X-Ray, he stopped short causing Greg Montgomery to run into him. Greg and Johnnie apologized to each other, and Johnnie directed him toward the booth.

Cookie delivered two plates and took two more orders. Mel introduced Greg to X-Ray.

Greg's hands trembled; and when he saw the others looking at them, he said, "Too much coffee. I got to reduce the caffeine," and chuckled nervously.

Mel recognized the signs of drug withdrawal, and it wasn't lost on X-Ray either, but the silence continued. Johnnie gave Mel a sign with his hands that Greg wasn't holding any drugs. Mel nodded her understanding and sighed.

After a time Mel broke the silence. "So, who goes first?"

X-Ray replied, "I do." He wiped his mouth on a paper napkin and dropped it ceremoniously on his near-empty plate. "Tell me about your friendship with Dee."

Greg put his hands in his lap and stared into space for a moment, then responded. "We met at a bar near the docks."

"When?" X-Ray asked.

"A couple of years back. Dee and Henry had been on-again-off-again in their marriage, but I don't think she was in the shelter yet."

"How'd you know she entered a shelter?" Johnnie asked.

"When she came to her first AA meeting about six months ago, I asked how she and Henry Lee were getting along. I liked her. I felt sorry for her and the way he treated her."

"How did you know he treated her?" X-Ray asked.

"I knew Henry Lee was a mean bastard by just the way he treated everyone there at the bar, but especially her. He bullied everyone. Even the bouncer quit taking him on. He slapped Dee around more than once. Pushed her down in her chair one time because she wanted to dance with someone else. I felt sorry for her.

"One night he really beat her. I don't remember why, if I ever knew. Anyway, several of us tried to pull him off her; but he gave me this and after that, I stayed back." He pointed to a small scar above his eyebrow.

"Where do you work?" Mel asked.

"I'm an orderly at Harbour View. I'm off today, but I've been checking in on her."

X-Ray spoke. "Wearing your white jacket and dark slacks, we thought you were just an employee stopping by to clean a patient's room."

"That too. But no. I went there in friendship." He paused. "Is she going to die?"

"We don't know yet. The outlook is grim," X-Ray replied.

"Did you ever meet Angel?" Mel asked.

126

"Yes. One time Dee couldn't find a babysitter and brought Angel to an AA meeting."

"Did you talk with the child?" X-Ray asked.

"No. Angel had some coloring books and earphones and a tape machine, so she kept to herself. That way she couldn't hear all of us sharing, you know."

"So, you never picked her up at school?" X-Ray asked.

"No, sir. I did not. I didn't even know where the shelter was located."

"You never followed her home?" Johnnie asked.

"Dee was very scared of Henry Lee finding her. I would never have put her in jeopardy by trying to follow her. I wouldn't take a chance of running into Henry Lee either." Greg rubbed the scar.

"Do you know how she got hurt?" X-Ray asked.

"No, sir, I don't." His shoulders quivered.

"Do you know WHO hurt her?"

"No, sir." Greg chewed on a nail bed that was already nibbled to the quick.

"Has she ever been in your car?" X-Ray leaned forward on his elbows and got right in Greg's face.

"No, sir."

"Are you sure?" X-Ray pressed on.

"Am I a suspect here? Do I need a lawyer?"

"Why do you think you need one?"

"You're acting very angry at me. I came here voluntarily... to answer some questions."

Mel patted the table in front of Greg, "That's all this is, answering some questions. No one's blaming anyone."

"When's the last time you saw her before her accident?" X-Ray disregarded Greg's fear and continued.

"At an AA meeting two weeks ago."

"Was she alone?"

"Yes."

"Did you talk?"

"Not alone. We stood in a group with a couple of other folks, and I got her a cup of coffee. We just talked about our work days, the weather, and such. Nothing specific."

"She didn't express any fear she might have had for her life?"

"If she did, she didn't share it with me or in the group."

"You have a crush on her, don't you?" Johnnie asked.

"I like her. I feel sorry for her. I'd like to help her."

Mel brought the interviewing to a close with, "We're all Dee's friends here, and we're all trying to help her."

"So, if you hear anything that might help us, you'll get in touch?" X-Ray pulled one of his cards from his jacket pocket and handed it to Greg. "Please call me – not either of these two – if you think of anything else."

Greg took the card. "I will, sir. I certainly will."

"And stay away from drugs. They'll kill you." X-Ray said, as he slid from the booth, dropped a few bills on the table, and walked out of the restaurant.

Mel paid the balance of the bill, then she and Greg and Johnnie left the restaurant.

"He's very smart, huh?" Greg asked the twosome.

"You mean about the drugs?" Johnnie said.

Mel turned to Greg and pointed her finger. "Tell us you didn't lie about Dee not only being in your car but bleeding on the headrest?"

Chapter Twenty-Eight

"I can't tell you. I'm afraid I'll get in trouble. You're scaring me." Greg backed away from the twosome toward the street.

"I'm gonna do more than scare you if you don't tell me the truth." Mel hollered at him, "You know cops, like attorneys, rarely ask questions they don't already know the answer to. Think about the questions Greg. Blood on the headrest. Following Dee. You'd better come clean."

"You can't make me," Greg screamed back. "He ran to his car, fumbled with his keys, then drove the rental car over the curb, and sped down the highway whipping the car back and forth in the lanes as he disappeared from view.

"I hope you're happy," Johnnie said.

"What does that mean?"

"You scared him off."

"When I get him, he's gonna wish he hadn't run away from me, much less lie to a sworn police officer."

"Why? What are you going to do? Follow him?"

"Me? Follow him? No way. For once – I'm gonna do my civic duty." Mel flipped the top on her phone and called X-Ray on the phone. She repeated Greg's conversation and gave X-Ray the description and license plate number of Greg's rental car, then tossed the phone into her purse.

"I'll teach him," Mel said, satisfied.

Johnnie followed Mel's car past the guard gate into her community and pulled in behind her as she parked in the garage. The smell of garlic and onions assailed their senses when they entered the hallway from the garage.

Both sniffed several times and smiled.

"Oh. Rosa prepared dinner," Mel said. She dropped her purse on the bottom riser of the staircase, kicked off her shoes, and walked into the kitchen. "She left us a note."

"Bless her heart," Johnnie said.

"What do you mean? You just ate."

"I can always eat. I smell something wonderful."

"It's pot roast," Mel said.

"I love that."

"Later, we have paperwork to do."

The phone rang. Mel picked up the hands-free and wandered toward her office.

"Hi, this is Mel."

"We got him," X-Ray said.

"Great. Johnnie and I'll be right down." She slipped into her shoes again.

"I don't think so."

She stopped in her tracks. "What do you mean?"

"You didn't play fair with me. I'm only reciprocating in kind."

"You love me like a sister."

"Who doesn't play fair and square and doesn't always share."

"Then why'd you call me?"

"I'm telling you we got him. I'm thanking you for being such a good citizen. Now let the police handle it."

"We can't interview him?"

"Nope. Not when he lies to me."

"The blood on the headrest was Dee's wasn't it?" Mel asked.

"I wasn't sure. The test results were faxed to me while we were chasing him down. Yes, they matched her blood and found her hair too."

"Boy, that pisses me off. Why would he hurt her?"

"You're on a 'need to know' for the time being."

"And I don't need to know?"

"Nope." X-Ray hung up.

Mel turned to Johnnie. "That isn't fair."

"Who said life was fair – lied."

The phone rang again.

Mel clicked it on. "I knew you'd change your mind."

"Mel. I guess you must be expecting another call. This is Sheriff Marshall calling. Am I interrupting anything?"

"Oh, hi. Not expecting a call, just hoping."

"Any change in Dee's condition?"

"No, she's still in a coma."

"I may have some news."

"Shoot."

"I found an unsigned hand-written note on my desk today that may concern Angel."

"What'd it say?"

"Don't give up. Look for her in the Big Thicket."

"What's that mean?"

"The Thicket is a kind of contemporary name. It's like really dense groves of titi that makes walking through the forest quite a challenge, if not impossible in some areas."

"How bad can a forest be?"

"Imagine thousands of acres of tall longleaf pines, hardwoods, blackjack, and post oaks. Lots of moss and wild critters."

"Does anyone live in there?"

"The Alabama-Coushatta Indians have a reservation in the middle of the Thicket. Why the cabin you stay in is part of the Thicket as is everyone else who lives near Boudin Lake."

"That sounds like a big task. What are you going to do about the note?"

"Gonna take a posse and look for her."

"Listen. Things are status quo here. I'll come down and help."

"Mel, the Indians call it the Big Bad Woods for a reason. Why, I've heard tales of thirty-foot long snakes, wild men running naked, carnivorous plants, black panthers. Why there's even talk of our own Big Foot – a kind of prehistoric half-man-half-animal roaming through there."

"Sounds like some tall Texas tales to me."

"Not trying to scare you. Not trying to get you here neither. Just checking in."

"Sheriff, my fear of flying is overshadowed by my desire to find Angel. I want to come. I won't get in the way. Really."

"It's very rugged. Can you ride a horse?"

"Sure, I can ride a horse."

How hard can that be, she thought to herself.

Johnnie laughed so hard he ran to the bathroom holding himself.

Chapter Twenty-Nine

Mel packed a couple of pairs of blue jeans, several bulky sweaters, a parka, and hiking boots stuffed with warm socks, and left a message on Lucas' cell phone that she'd be flying into Beaumont, not Houston, for her rental unit. She wasn't going to take a chance with another rental unit so far away from its Houston base.

She grabbed a bite of Rosa's pot roast right out of the pan before leaving for John Wayne Airport and stuffed an extra bottle of water in her backpack.

Johnnie dropped her off at the airport still chuckling. As she exited the car, he hollered to her, "Did you bring something for chafing?"

"What's that mean?" she said in bafflement, as Johnnie drove off in the Mustang.

She changed planes in Houston for the short hop to the Beaumont airport. In baggage, she retrieved her luggage and rolled it toward the local car rental agency aisle when she spotted a familiar person.

"Hello, Gina. What are you doing here?"

"Hi. Mama and Sheriff suggested I pick you up. You aren't really going to need a car."

"I know. I have a horse."

"Oh, that too. But you can drive Jimmy."

"That's very thoughtful of you. Did Slim ever come back from vacation?"

Mel followed Gina outside the terminal toward the covered parking lot.

"Back and gone again," Gina said.

"Does he ever really work?"

"Sort of. He's a widower, so he works until he gets bait, food, and fuel for his boat engine; then he's off again fishing."

"Did he ever get the rental car fixed?"

"No. I heard Sheriff tell my mom those rental folks came with a tow truck and took it away."

"That's good. I haven't received my bill yet on that fiasco, so I don't know what that's going to run me."

They walked down several parking lanes and parked against the wall was the Jimmy and a recognizable trailer even by city-slicker standards.

Mel laughed. "Is this where I get my first riding lesson?"

Gina chuckled, "No Ma'am. Sheriff asked me to pick up a couple of horses that he'd ordered. One for you and an extra." She held one end of the luggage and helped Mel toss the luggage into the truck's bed. Mel added her backpack, then walked around to the rear of the trailer.

"Well, hello..." she knelt down to look between their rear haunches, "girls. Which one is mine?"

Gina smiled and replied, "Here's your first equine lesson. Those are fellas...without the mating equipment. We call 'em geldings."

Mel stood proudly, patted them both once, and walked toward the passenger door. "I knew that."

"Uh huh," Gina said.

They stopped off at City Hall. Joanna came around her desk and hugged Mel. "I'm glad to see you. Although for the life of me, I don't know why you'd leave the comfort of a nice warm, dry bed and want to join the search."

"Because I made a promise to Dee."

"I know that about you. You're good people. Is there any change at all in Dee's condition?"

"No, I'm sorry to report, she's still unconscious. No real life signs at all."

"As long as her heart is beating, her will is strong. I'm praying for her every day."

"She could sure use prayer."

"Sheriff wanted me to tell you the cabin will be the staging area for the search." She turned away and shuffled through several papers on her desk. "One more thing..."

Her fax machine began to spew out papers. The phone rang. The sound of several pickup trucks skidding to a stop on the gravel parking lot interrupted her sentence. The front door flew open, and Sheriff led the way, as the room filled with men carrying rifles and walkie-talkies, and wearing holsters with sidearms.

"Did you hear?" Sheriff said.

"No, I don't have the radio on," Joanna replied.

He pointed toward the fax machine. "That'll be their photos. Huntsville had a breakout at the Ellis Unit."

Mel interjected, "Does this happen often?"

"You mean that guy that held you and Gina hostage? Naw. He was harmless, just walked off a nearby pea farm prison.

These are the bad guys. Ellis One houses all the death row inmates."

"Where is it located?" Mel asked.

"Fifteen miles or so north of Huntsville." He leaned in for emphasis, "Real close to where we're standing right now."

Mel felt a chill chase her spine to the ground, and she shifted her legs nervously.

The sheriff walked to the fax, took the papers, and pinned them side-by-side on a cork-board against the back wall. The men moved in closer as the sheriff continued. "Okay, we got two guys... killers... both of them. Won't be caught alive. This is what I know." He took a paper from his shirt pocket and read. "This is the first escape from Texas' death row since the Bonnie and Clyde gang charged into the Eastman Unit with guns blazing and broke out Barrow's cousin. What was his name?" The sheriff scratched his head.

Gina spoke. "It was in January 1934, sir. Clyde's cousin was named Raymond Hamilton. He was serving a 263-year sentence for bank robberies."

"Thank you, Gina," Sheriff replied. "I knew I could depend on you."

Gina added, "They recaptured Hamilton and sentenced him to die for killing a guard during that escape. A few months later, he escaped again, but this time from the 'Walls' unit. The Rangers tracked him down, and the State executed him in 1935."

"Thank you, honey. So, you know they ain't happy at the 'Walls' right now."

The men mumbled in agreement.

Gina whispered to Mel, "The 'Walls' is what they call the old main prison in downtown Huntsville. You should see those high walls. Thick, really tall, a real dreary red-colored brick."

The sheriff continued, "Three more death row inmates scaled the wires. When they jumped to the ground, the guards spotted them and fired at them. They gave up."

The group gave a collective, "All right."

"Now we got two to catch. How they cleared that razor-wire-topped perimeter fence and avoided getting shot, I'll never know," Sheriff said to no one in particular.

One of the men answered, "They got lucky. But that won't last long."

"Let me read what the report says for you," Sheriff said. "Prison officials believe the inmates stuffed pillows and blankets in their beds ahead of time to make it appear that they were asleep in their cells. Then they hid somewhere outside the prison when a scheduled recreation break ended.

"Officials found a broken door in the recreation area and a segment of fence where they'd peeled it back enough to slip through. They found discarded prison uniforms and some black felt pens."

Someone asked, "What's the pens for?"

Sheriff answered, "To make it harder for guards to spot them in the dark and in the forest, they dyed their white underwear black. Anyway, a guard spotted them jumping from the roof and sounded the alarm. Then all hell broke loose."

Another asked, "Did either of them get hit at least?"

Sheriff answered as he read the report, "Looks like some blood found at the drop site." He slapped the paper with one hand and scanned the small audience of hunters. "You know this Marty guy," he pointed to one of the photos, "killed a Texas Ranger."

The noise and body odors in the cramped room rose to a level that reminded Mel of her beloved Dallas Cowboys in a huddle against their biggest rival. They were one pumped-up bunch.

"Okay, so we have a lot of help." The sheriff read on. "The Rangers are bringing out everything: boats, dogs, trucks, helicopters, cars, checking the main highways, side roads, and trails, all vacations and leaves canceled, and the horses of course. Which reminds me, fellas, this is Mel from California, who ISN'T going on this search?" Without looking at Mel, he pointed in a jabbing dismissing way at her.

The guys turned, nodded, "Hello," and removed their hats.

"Oh yes, I am. I haven't come this far to miss this. Anyway, if this is anywhere near the Big Thicket, we'll have two searches…the bad guys AND to look for Angel." She held up two fingers for emphasis.

One of the men turned around to Mel, "It's all Big Thicket, Ma'am."

"I ain't got time to argue with no filly," the sheriff summarily dismissed her comments, turned to the wall, picked up a ruler, and pulled down a grid sheet from the ceiling. "Okay guys," he slapped the map with the ruler and began to draw lines as he spoke. "The Trinity River runs here along the back side of the prison. We got piney woods on both sides of Farm-to-Market Road 980. That's the main road to the prison. The Rangers assigned us these grids. Joanna, you gotta marker?"

Joanna opened her desk drawer, withdrew a yellow pen, and tossed it to the sheriff.

"Okay," he looked at the paper the prison had faxed, then colored the areas, and continued to talk. "This is a tough area."

One man spoke up, "Sheriff, that's more than tough. It's very dense in there. Lots of swampy bogs, quicksand, snakes, and shit."

"Don't you guys have some cadaver dogs? Some thermal-seeking devices? A GPS?" Mel asked.

Collectively, the group of men turned to Mel. A bold one spoke, "Ma'am, we got bloodhounds, our rifles, a compass, and our balls. That's all we need."

Everyone laughed except Mel, who faded into the background at his response.

"If it was easy, they'd have asked some other team to do it. Now we don't want any bounty hunters here. No hot doggers. Is everybody happy with this duty? Happy with everybody here?"

The hand-full of men looked around the room, acknowledged each other, nodded, and replied, "Yes."

"Okay, raise your right hand."

As the sheriff deputized the group, Mel raised her right hand too – the only woman in the room to do so.

Chapter Thirty

"Are you bothered by flies here?" Mel asked Gina, as they got into the Jimmy.

"Flies?" Gina laughed. "You got a lot more to worry about than that in the thicket. "We got mosquitoes big enough to carry a man away. We got sand fleas and tiny flying things that will eat your legs and ankles alive. The whelps they leave behind will drive you crazy. My advice is don't scratch 'em. We got poisonous snakes, fire ants, alligators...."

"What's the good news?" Mel interrupted.

"If you're seriously going to do this, we gotta do some shopping. There's no drinkable water out there; and you'll need extra food, a rain coat, a tent, bedding, some toilet tissue, lotion for the bites, and something for chaffing."

Mel and Gina drove into Lufkin to the nearest large shopping area and bought supplies, then returned to Zavalla. Recent heavy rains had left deep runny ruts in the road, and the truck slipped and skidded all the way from the main highway to the cabin.

As they bounced toward the end of the drive, Mel said, "I

wonder how I'm going to carry everything we bought and my makeup bag and all."

Gina said, "You won't have to worry about that bag."

"Why is that?"

The Jimmy skidded to a halt at the rear of a truck in a long line of campers and trucks that led to the cabin.

"I can see you've never been on a hunt. Come on. You'll see."

A puzzled Mel followed Gina as they passed the vehicles. There in the opening men filed their nails and sipped on coffee over an open fire. Just outside the lean-to, Joanna stood behind a man sitting on a tree stump. She held a comb in one hand and a razor in the other.

"That's why," Gina said, as she pointed to her mother.

"Next?" Joanna said. The bald man stood, rubbed his head, and swaggered toward the fire. Another man with long black hair he had tied with a leather strip, removed his knit cap, crunched it between his large fists, and followed the previous customer to the stump-seat.

"Oh no. I'm not going to shave my head," Mel said.

The sheriff exited the cabin in time to hear that and said, "I'm glad to hear that. You'll be my deputy-at-home. You stay here and give me hourly reports from Huntsville."

"I'll do no such thing." An angry Mel played with the curls that swirled about the nape of her neck. "I'm here to find Angel. You play cops and robbers. We just happen to be on the same trail at the same time."

"Hair's gotta go, most of it anyway. Are those nails real?"

She glanced at them, her fingers splayed in front of her. "Yeah, why?"

"Gotta go, too. Down to the quick. Don't want any nails

ripped off and bleed around the hounds. It ain't your period is it?"

Highly indignant now, Mel replied, "What's that got to do with hunting?"

"Alligators love fresh blood," Gina whispered.

The men chuckled.

"No," she spoke loudly, "that's not a problem for me."

"Good. Line up for your buzz. You're next after Buck here."

Mel negotiated with Joanna, who gave Mel a military buzz, leaving some on top.

"This is for your own good, Mel," Joanna said.

"My mother used to say that when she was giving me some really bad medicine."

"We can't have hair get caught in the brush and rip your scalp off. There's no time for grooming, and by the way, how's your shots?"

"I had my tetanus last time I was here. Remember?"

"File your nails. Then Gina will show you how to pack your things and saddle your horse. You have met your horse, haven't you?"

"We met at the airport."

"He's very tame."

"That's good. What's his name?"

"We call him Dizzy, but his real name is Destroyer."

Chapter Thirty-One

A heavy mist settled in around the cabin. The dozen or so men set up their tents, cooked dinner, cleaned up afterward, fed and watered their horses, then gathered around a large campfire.

Gina and Mel ate the red beans, rice, and cornbread dinner with the men. Later, Gina introduced Mel to Dizzy.

"He's beautiful." She rubbed his shiny black coat. "How do I steer this thing?" Mel asked.

Gina chuckled, "Sheriff said you knew how to ride."

"I lied. How hard can it be?"

"It's pretty easy, actually." Gina demonstrated by grabbing the reins on the left side, placing her left foot into a stirrup, and hoisting herself onto Dizzy's back. The horse remained perfectly still.

"That looks pretty easy."

"Want to try it?"

"Naw. I'll be fine."

"Then to go left, pull on the left rein, ditto the right. Pull back when you want to stop, and spur him with your heels when you want to go."

"That's just like driving a car."

"Well, not exactly. Mel, are you sure you want to do this?"

"Sure. Angel may be out there. It's a promise I made to Dee. I'm tough. My dad was a cop for God's sake."

"I don't mean to simplify the situation, but he was a 'city' cop. This is a lot different."

"Me and Dizzy, we're going to get along just fine. We're going to bring Angel back too. I feel like John Wayne."

Gina shook her head, rolled her eyes, and sighed. They fed Dizzy and covered him with a blanket, then entered the cabin where Gina gave the most simple, specific folding and packing instructions Mel had ever heard. If you can't wear everything, don't take it. Direct.

The sheriff held court with last minute advice.

"Is everybody ready?" He asked.

A collective "Yes" whispered through the group.

"Settle in then. Two o'clock comes early."

Mel turned to Gina and whispered, "Two a.m.?"

Gina walked down the lane to the Jimmy, and without a smile, waved, and replied over her shoulder, "You'll get used to it. Good luck."

The smell of strong coffee from the front yard caused Mel to stir. She yawned, stretched, groomed, and dressed warmly. She rubbed her near-bald head and vowed to wear a hat until the hair grew back. She pulled on a lipstick-red parka and a red knit cap bought at the urging of Gina, who assured her the bright color would, at least, keep someone from mistaking Mel for an animal and shooting her accidentally in the brush.

She pulled her hiking boots on over heavy woolen socks and laced them to the top grommet, then pulled her jean legs down over the boots. She felt like the Michelin Man, full-bodied and barely able to walk.

After a hardy breakfast, the sheriff called everyone around the campfire.

"Okay. This morning's report from Huntsville remains unchanged since yesterday afternoon. Eighteen hours and both escapees are still on the loose. The Rangers and their teams have surrounded Ellis."

"How big an area is that?" Mel asked.

"The prison complex is, ah, I suspect over eleven thousand acres."

"Whew. That's a lot of bad people," Mel said to no one in particular.

A man who stood next to her said, "It's Rangers, dogs, horses, and long-range rifles. No one's gonna outrun a couple of Rangers and their horses, nor the killer dogs. That's why most prisons in Texas don't even have fences. You can't outrun a bullet."

The sheriff continued, "They're going to concentrate their search efforts on the six-square-mile area south and east of the Unit."

The man nudged Mel and whispered, "The men would be plain stupid to stay in there. That place is crawling with snakes, big poisonous ones, and alligators that are real hungry because there's little food to harvest in that area."

A chill ran down Mel's back.

Everyone received their final instructions and grid assignments. Men faded back and forth through the thick fog as they checked the batteries in the walkie-talkies, loaded their equipment on horses or in truck beds, mounted up and drove off.

Gina had shown Mel how to load Dizzy with equipment equally dispersed in two leather saddlebags: one on each side of his rear haunch.

Sheriff introduced Mel to a grizzly-faced old guy named Ziggy and his two dogs, Maggie May and Get'em. Mel tried not to laugh. Ziggy wasn't thrilled to meet Mel either.

He muttered as he loaded the dogs onto the back of his truck. He placed Get'em in a cage. Maggie May lay near the tailgate. "I ain't never been on no hunt with no gal before." Then louder for Mel's ears, "If you get behind with Dizzy, you get behind, just give Dizzy his reins. He'll take you home. You ain't holding us back. When these dogs get the scent, they're gonna run like hell. You don't catch up, you gonna be awfully lost in that nasty thicket. I ain't comin' back for ya, little lady. Me and the dogs, we gotta a job to do."

Mel patted her horse's head. "How fast?" She asked.

"They can track from anywhere to twelve to twenty-two miles a day. They're very fast runners."

She cringed at the thought of galloping through the forest.

In an attempt to warm Ziggy to her going on the hunt, she knelt and put her hands out to Maggie May. The proud and noble bloodhound stood and walked up to Mel, smelled her, and licked her face. Mel patted Maggie May's brown and black fur and the elegant bump on her head, then rubbed each long ear that flopped lower than her heavily wrinkled face and jowls. "She beautiful."

"Thanks," Ziggy replied.

"Tell me about her."

"She's so good at tracking that her testimony holds up in court."

"No kidding. That's terrific. How does this tracking thing work?"

This became Ziggy's opportunity to shine. "See those ears?

I give her the scented item. She captures the smell there in her large olfactory system – that long nose. The scent flows to those long ears. As they flop in the breeze, the scent goes to the wrinkles and stays there a while. And when she's running, she drools; and that keeps the scent active a lot longer."

"How does she know she's going hunting?"

"I told her we had a job and showed her the lead this morning. When she does a good job, she gets a cookie."

"Otherwise she never gets cookies?"

"That's right."

"Bought her for a dollar. She's four now and the best damn tracker in the business."

"She appears to be a very social animal," Mel said.

"Yeah, unlike Get'em."

Mel leaned over to Get'em's cage and held out her hand to him. His refined and chiseled head and pointed ears defined his character. He bared his teeth and growled and snapped as angry as Mel had seen a mad dog get. She jumped back. "Jesus."

"I should have warned you. Get'em is the biter. He don't like nobody. He just catches people."

"So, one tracks, and the other captures?" Mel asked.

"A lover and a fighter – that's their roles."

"He's a pretty shepherd."

"He's a Belgian Malinois."

Get'em barked so angrily that Ziggy said something Mel couldn't make out, and the dog stopped barking.

"What'd you tell him?"

"He speaks only Dutch. I told him to shut up. Properly trained, he has ten million times the sensitivity of human smell."

"Wow. I got to keep up with these two? Okay, here I go."

Mel squared her shoulders and worked at mounting her horse. She could hardly get her left foot into the stirrup. *It looked so easy last night,* she thought.

The second step was hoisting her full body weight up on Dizzy's back. That took several attempts. Dizzy must have sensed she hadn't ridden before and that caused him to turn his head and check her out. He also stepped sideways several times, and her left foot missed the stirrup.

"Easy boy," Mel said. "We can do this."

Dizzy bucked a bit with both front legs pawing at the air. Mel walked to his head and whispered in one ear, "I don't know how long we're going to be together, so please let's just make the most of it."

Dizzy gave her a horse laugh.

Both final moves caused her to breathe heavy. But at least she was astride Dizzy. She patted him for comfort: hers and his. "Thank you," she told him.

Ziggy shook his head, jammed some tobacco in the back of his lower gums, jumped into the cab of the truck; and they were off.

Before they reached the main highway, Mel's butt and inside thighs were sore. It seemed to her that every time Dizzy moved down in one of those hard ruts, her butt flew into the air. Every time he moved up to a dirt mound, her butt hit the saddle.

"Oh Lord, help me," was all she could say, as she and Dizzy followed Ziggy's truck and horse trailer.

She kept Dizzy on the unpaved shoulder of the road and followed the long trail of taillights and horses. Several riders fell in behind Mel causing her to keep up with the pack.

Mel leaned over and whispered to Dizzy, "I hope to hell

you know where we're going, 'cause I sure don't."

Dizzy let out with another horse neigh and jerked at the reins. It was his way of telling Mel she was gripping the reins so hard the bit was cutting into his mouth.

"Take it easy on old Dizzy," someone behind her called out.

She said, "Thank you," and tried to relax for the next what seemed like a hundred miles when they reached their grid.

Miles and miles of pine trees lined the highway. The long-leaf pines and cypresses stood like sentinels so close together that Mel thought they'd been planted that way. Thick ivy, ferns, kudzu, and dying tree limbs cluttered what available ground remained.

She hoped it was a mirage, and that at daylight this scene wouldn't be so dense. A few minutes after four, the trucks stopped and turned off their headlights. The area pitched into darkness so deep that Mel couldn't see either her hand in front of her or Dizzy's head. Dizzy shuddered beneath her loins. Somewhere in the fog, a generator whelped into action, and spotlights lit the area. The hunters checked their gear, tightened and released their tack, then mounted the horses, and lined up to enter the forest.

Ziggy joined them. He put leads on the dogs as they jumped from the truck, Maggie May's long ears flopped in the breeze; Get'em's ears pointed skyward. They sniffed the grounds around the forest edge, peed on several trees, then squatted and left large deposits behind.

"Is that so they can find their way back to the truck?" Mel asked.

"Naw. We don't teach 'em to backtrack. They just had to pee and crap." He laughed at Mel.

Maybe I should do the same, Mel thought.

Chapter Thirty-Two

Considerable chatter among the men filled the narrow two-lane farm-to-market road. Echoes bounced off the asphalt and in between the two stands of trees and brush. Mel asked Ziggy, "Are we going to be here long enough for me to get off?"

"Dismount?" Ziggy asked.

"What?"

"Do you mean you want to dismount?"

"Yeah, I think that's what I want to do."

"Sure. We can't get started until the helicopter arrives and that won't be till daylight. And we need a Ranger, and they don't rise early like us."

"How long do you think?" Mel asked.

Ziggy looked at the sky. Thirty minutes for daylight maybe, unless that storm brings us a lot of cloud cover."

"How do you know a storm is coming?"

"Inhale."

Mel took one long breath and smelled something sharp and pungent. "What is that?"

"Ozone's a clear sign of rain."

Mel dismounted and tied Dizzy's reins to a nearby tree so he could roam and munch on grass. She patted him on the rump like she saw other riders do to their mounts. She rubbed her already sore inner thighs and walked bowlegged to the back of the truck where Ziggy stood.

"Do I get a gun?" Mel asked.

"You mean a rifle?" Ziggy replied.

"Whatever. Do I get to carry a weapon of any kind?"

"No. You got me and Frank and Larry and the dogs. We three are all crack shots."

Mel wished she had, at least, packed Gina's gun that she had hid in the cabin after her previous visit. She flipped out her cell phone and started to dial.

"What are you doing?" Ziggy asked.

"Calling my office."

"Now look at those trees, little lady. Both sides of the highway. We're in the Big Thicket, thousands of acres of stands of lumber for hundreds of miles in all directions, much taller than seventy-five, hundred feet maybe. How you think a signal gonna catch you here? Honestly," Ziggy shook his head in disdain.

She pocketed the phone. "Okay, so what's our plan?" she asked.

He rubbed his day-old stubble and replied, "Your California crime unit sent me some of Angel's dirty clothes and her bed linens. I cut 'em up into pieces and divided them among all the teams what's got dogs."

"Why are we following the scent from this point?"

"Because we're really close to the Boudreaux place for one thing. Number two, we've found bodies in this area before. It's kind of a dumping ground, if you know what I mean, for the Boudreaux clan."

"Oh."

"So, you don't think Angel will be alive?"

Ziggy gave her a look, sat down on the bed of his open tailgate, and wrapped some rope into loops between his elbow and palms without responding to her.

Mel spotted the Jimmy coming down the road. Joanna pulled over to the shoulder and jumped out of the driver's side. "Good morning, Mel."

"Why in God's name would anyone, who didn't have to – get up this early?"

Joanna walked to the truck bed and grabbed a low-cut cardboard box and hoisted it over the bed. She rested it on the edge of the fender-well and hollered to everyone, "Donuts and coffee."

Sheriff reached the truck first and, towering over Joanna by at least a foot, leaned over and kissed Joanna on her head. "Bless your heart," he said. He yanked the box by the sides and carried it over to Ziggy's open tailgate. He snatched a jelly one for himself and with a mouth-full said, "Oh, this will go down better with some of Opal's hot coffee."

Joanna had a large coffee urn and paper cups ready for the group, and they swamped her with thanks all around. She stood back as each man waited on himself.

"Some guy named Johnnie from your office called the sheriff's office."

"Yeah? Is Dee awake?"

"There's no change in her condition. He said he couldn't reach you on your cell and was concerned about you."

"Did you tell him I'm going on the hunt today?"

"Yes...listen, are you sure you want to do this?" Joanna asked.

"I know it's much more comfortable in the cabin," Mel said and smiled.

"At least it'd be dry and warm. That's more than I can hope for you out here. Weatherman out of Beaumont said one hundred percent chance of thundershowers throughout the week."

"Thanks, but I made a promise; and if Angel is here, I want to be the one to bring her back to Dee. Anyway, we're waiting for the copter and a Ranger right now," Mel informed Joanna.

"I know. Ranger's right behind me a couple of miles. The copter..."

Sounds of whirring blades in the far distance gave a clear explanation to the remainder of Joanna's sentence.

Everyone looked skyward and waited. The whipping sounds neared; and the winds began to swirl violently flicking up debris and knocking off hats, as the shiny black machine cleared the treetops and landed on the road. The horses and dogs got spooked and began to dart back and forth with apprehension. Joanna dashed to the truck to cover the remaining donuts from flying debris.

A white four-door sedan sped down the highway also towing a horse trailer. It skidded to a stop on the gravel shoulder, and small pebbles and dust filled the air around the group that stood nearby. "That'll be the Ranger," Ziggy said to Mel. "Come on. Sheriff has last minute instructions for us."

Everyone knew their job – to find Angel and capture the two escapees. Mel hoped it'd be in that order so she could go home early with happy news.

Daylight broke with rumbling thunder in the distance. Gray clouds boiled across the highway, and it began to sprinkle. Mel found her rain slicker wrapped around the outside of one saddle bag and slipped it on.

"That's my cue," Joanna said. "If you change your mind, give Dizzy his head; and he'll take you back to the cabin. Me or Gina will check in with Sheriff from time-to-time if any of you need us. Stay safe out there." She waved and drove off.

She shook hands with the balance of her team: Frank and Larry, young twins who spoke, nodded, and removed their hats for her simultaneously.

They stood over six-feet tall, lanky, with matching black boots, jeans, and orange vests over parkas. She could distinguish one from the other because Frank had the slightest hint of a dark mustache on his upper lip. Larry's baby face shined like it had been freshly scrubbed, pink cheeks and all from the cool morning air.

They checked their gear and saddles, then mounted their horses. Ziggy gave the dogs several whiffs of the material he had withdrawn from a paper bag inside a plastic bag. The dogs wailed, sniffed the grounds anxiously, and disappeared into the thick underbrush. Ziggy followed them with Frank, then Mel, and Larry rapidly bringing up the flank.

Once they moved into the forest a few feet, Mel turned in her saddle. She could no longer see anything but forest. It's as if the trees had swallowed her group whole. She was in the belly of the Big Thicket. Her hands shook, and she rested them on the saddle-horn to calm herself. Rain fell more rapid now bringing down with it leaves and twigs from above. A pine cone dropped on her shoulder, and she jumped. Even Dizzy felt the nervousness on his back, as he turned his head, his black eyes stared at her. Larry's horse trotted a bit faster and caught up with Mel.

"If you're spooked, you'll spook your horse."

"It's not that. I'm just not used to being out of control. I'm not in my environment, and this is a bit unsettling."

"You can always go home. I'll take you back," he offered.

"No." She patted Dizzy's black neck and said, "I'll be fine."

She began her internal mantra, *find Angel. Find Angel alive. Find Angel for Dee.*

Chapter Thirty-Three

Rain continued to drizzle through the trees as they drove farther and farther away from civilization. No one spoke, and Mel soon picked up sounds; a bird, then several that telephoned back and forth spreading the news that strangers had invaded their forest. Water splats, squirrels scampered across the forest floor in search of food for their winter storage, pine cones dropped to make new trees, dead limbs slammed to the ground for someone else's firewood on a much dryer morning. Mel was wonder-struck by these new sounds and discoveries.

The dogs ran out of sight several times only to slow down and wait until Mel and Larry caught up. Lightning struck nearby. Everyone's horses jumped, and Mel looked to make sure nothing caught fire.

"Too damp in this area for a fire," Ziggy called out to Mel.

This pattern continued for most of the morning. Mel could hear the other groups on either side of them, but because of the concentrated foliage, she couldn't see anyone. Not one to complain, especially around the rugged men, when her stomach growled, she ignored it. Her hands remained dry under the space lined material of the gloves that Gina insisted she buy. *What a good investment*, Mel thought, as she removed one glove and reached into her parka pocket for some trail mix.

At several points in the journey, Ziggy and Frank got off their horses and hacked away at the impenetrable underbrush with machetes. Various shades of green legumes, forbs, and tangle grasses stood knee-to-shoulder high and in many areas brushed almost to Mel's knees. By noon, Mel saw more light just ahead, and they broke through the forest into a large opening filled with blackened stubs of reddish-brown tree trunks. Ziggy suggested they dismount and rest. He gave the dogs and all the horses water. Everyone poured coffee from their thermos.

"Looks like a fire struck here," Mel said.

"It's all part of a controlled burn we had. Extends for miles."

Mel looked left, then right, "How deep?"

"We'll stay in it until lunch. We'll eat before we get back into the hunt."

"How can we start a fire in this weather?"

"We don't. Eat cold for lunch, hot for dinner. If we keep making time today, we'll bunk near the old sawmill tonight. Is that all right with everyone?"

Larry and Frank nodded. Mel said, "Whatever. That's fine with me."

Ziggy looked at the ground, got on his haunches and picked at something with his fingers, then smelled.

"We got a cat here. Probably not more than twenty minutes ahead of us." He stood and pointed, "And going our way."

The dogs paced the ground, and Ziggy gave them another

sniff at the material. They ran ahead.

"I like cats, although I'm allergic to their fur," Mel said nonchalantly.

"It ain't that kinda cat," Ziggy said without looking at Mel. He took his rifle out of the scabbard and checked the ammo, then replaced it in the holster.

"I knew that," she said to no one in particular, then remounted Dizzy.

Ziggy put his fingers together and whistled with a shrillness that echoed through the forest and hurt Mel's ears. The dogs bounced back to his side within a minute or two. Ziggy talked with them, then with hand motions sent them back to their task.

"Like they understand you," Mel said.

"They better. Their lives depend on it."

A fog horn sound roared in the distance.

"They got one of the convicts," Frank said.

"How do you know that?" Mel asked.

"We're trackers. It's what we do."

"How do you know it isn't Angel they found?"

"It'd be a different noise."

Mel remained ambivalent about the crudeness of the telegraphing between groups, yet she asked anyway. "What is the sound if they find Angel and...she's not alive?"

"You don't want to know."

No one spoke until Ziggy motioned for them to stop and dismount at the edge of the burned area. The dogs circled the area panting.

"Everyone grab something to eat. Mel if you need to use the bathroom, just two important points: don't get out of our sight and don't wipe with soft pointed leaves that grow in groups of three on a bush with pretty grayish-looking berries."

"Why is that?"

"That's poison ivy. Only thing worse than chafing is poison ivy or poison oak."

Ziggy whistled and laid out some food and water bowls for the dogs. He fed his horse and wiped him down with a chamois. Mel found her cloth and repeated the process for Dizzy. He appeared grateful and tried to grab the rag and nudged her bit.

"He likes you," Frank said.

"Right," Mel replied.

Despite the weather, sweat ran down the inside of her thighs; and they now slightly tingled. When she found an area partially protected from the men, she lowered her jeans to discover both areas red with whelps. She removed a can of white salve and rubbed it on both thighs. She flinched because the wiping action caused the area to sting. She dabbed the spots with toilet tissue and pulled up her jeans.

The dogs ran to her area, sniffed in circles, and made their deposits to cover hers.

"They're protecting the human scent. Right now we're tracking the cat. Don't want the cat to circle around and track us. They know the scent of a woman."

"Oh, that's comforting."

They stood in a semi-circle and ate jerky, trail mix, and nuts, and chased it all with now lukewarm coffee and water from their thermos bottles, then mounted to continue their journey.

Mel thought, *find Angel. Find Angel alive. Find Angel for Dee.*

She had gotten used to the forest sounds, and like bored youngsters on a long road trip, made a game of trying to identify each noise. The horses now wheezed a bit. Their breath white in the afternoon coolness. Twigs crunched under the clip-clopping of their hoofs. After riding for a few hours, the dog sounds, which had been a consistent yapping-type clamor that she recognized, suddenly reached a high pitch yelp. Frank spurred his horse that ran like a stallion out of a starting gate and disappeared ahead as did Larry.

"What is it?" Mel asked when she and Dizzy caught up.

"It's something," Larry replied.

"Alive or dead?"

"I'll know when I get there," he said.

Chapter Thirty-Four

The two horses ran quite a distance into the grove until they reached the area where the dogs had stopped.

Larry motioned for Mel to remain on her mount. He grabbed his rifle, slipped off his horses' back, and approached the scene immediately ahead of them. The men stood around something deep in the underbrush. Their rifles remained slung over their shoulders, but with fingers on the triggers. Mel anxiously strained in the stirrups to catch sight of the object. Ziggy had brushed some dead leaves away with the toe of his boot, ordered the dogs to stand down, then knelt beside the mound, and touched it.

Larry returned to Mel. He took a burlap bag from his storage along with a large hunting knife.

"What is it?"

"Dinner," he dryly replied, as he walked back to Ziggy and Frank.

After twelve hours in the saddle, Mel felt more like Billy Crystal than John Wayne. Between her sore thighs, aching back, and numb butt, she was ready to sleep anywhere. She just didn't know where that would be.

The rain had slowed during the afternoon; and now only dampness and the smell of ozone, ferns, pine trees, and sweaty horses remained. Mel had defined another noise; that of the deep, resonant, thrumming sounds the hundred-foot pines made in a high wind. The air current had definitely picked up, but blissfully the thunder had stopped.

The mist appeared to lift briefly, and through the greenery, some low square stumps covered with moss, ivy, and pine needles came into view. The horses walked down a lane of brown straw needles between the twenty or so seat-like structures. As they neared, Mel saw the moss covered concrete, not wood, with white blotches all around them.

A two-story block building with no windows or doors, and in some areas, no roof, stood at the end of the lane. Dampness had aged the building; and it reminded her of England's Stonehenge, only shorter and without mystery once Ziggy explained when he dismounted.

"These ruins were once an active sawmill."

"How'd the logs get here?"

"By rail, in and out." He pointed to a distant point. But all Mel saw were tree trunks and green leaves.

"We'll bed down here for the night. Who wants first shift?"

"For what?"

"Animals and bad guys."

"Oh. I'll take the first if you give me a rifle," Mel offered.

"No. I always sit first," Ziggy said. "Frank, you take two and Larry three. If there's any time left, wake Mel up. Let's unload." His walkie-talkie crackled, and he walked away from the building for better reception.

Mel watched the guys as they set up camp. Following their

actions, she pulled her pup-tent and bedroll off Dizzy and set up her bed. As she selected dry clothes for the following morning, she found a surprise stuffed inside one leg of clean jeans – Gina's gun, with an extra clip. *Bless her heart*, Mel thought, as she placed everything inside the tent.

Ziggy had left, and she assumed it was to use the bathroom. He returned with his arms full of firewood.

"You guys bring in more so we can keep it going all night. Cats hate fires."

Mel caught up with Larry, who carried a small shovel, and said, "After all this rain and dampness, how are we going to find dry wood?"

"You lift up the top forest layer that's damp, and get that just below – but not what's on the ground. Think of it as a bed. What'll burn is not the blanket on top or the bed cover over the mattress, but the top sheet in between."

"Got it."

Mel stirred pine needles near a stand of wood with her foot, then reached down to lift up a large area. Beneath that she discovered a small group of white and brown shiny mushrooms. She plucked one, wiped it off with her sleeve, and was about to pop it in her mouth when Larry hit her in the back causing her to drop the cap.

"Never. I repeat, NEVER eat a mushroom cap growing under pine trees. They are deadly."

"Oh," she replied meekly, as she wiped her hands on her jeans. "I am very sorry to be so much trouble."

"You're no trouble really; you're just naive. Tomorrow we're gonna move fast and early because we've got to clear the bogs before the alligators get up. They'll be hungry."

While dinner cooked, they removed the saddles, fed

and bedded the horses and dogs. Dizzy appeared to quiver in comfort when she laid a blanket across his back. Frank skinned, then skewered the deer carcass over the roaring fire, boiled water for the instant food bags, and brewed hot coffee in a black metal kettle. Larry dug a hole and, after the meal, laid the remains inside and buried it. The venison tasted gamey to Mel, but no one complained, and she didn't either. Twelve hours astride a horse's back will do that to you.

They retired to their tents while Frank stood watch. He walked the perimeter of their camp, smoked a cigarette, and cradled his rifle. Mel said, "Goodnight," crawled into her tent, and changed clothes. She lay her head down and was asleep before she pulled up her blanket.

Mel slept despite the hard damp ground. She had no idea the time of night or morning, when she heard two men hollering something at each other, a brief scuffle followed, then a shot rang out that echoed across the woodland. The walkie-talkie came alive with chatter.

"Ziggy," Sheriff hollered through the unit, "Answer me Ziggy. Are you and Mel all right?"

Chapter Thirty-Five

Mel slipped her boots on and tied the laces tight enough for her to run if she had to. She tried not to touch the tent so her movement couldn't be detected.

Muffled voices, angry and defiant, filled the night's silence. The sheriff continued to call out for a response over the walkie-talkie. She decided to step out and face the music. With gun in hand, she unzipped the tent and stood.

The darkness shielded her, and she could see a large man, whose back was to her, holding a rifle on her three companions and screaming at them.

She thought it was the escapee from Huntsville until Ziggy spotted her and with his hands high in the air said, "Now Henry Lee Boudreaux, you know me. Our families go way back. You know I got no bone to pick with you. Me and the boys we're out here looking for that escaped convict." Ziggy took one step forward and added, "Of course, if you want to show us where we can find Angel that'd be a real coup. And we wouldn't tell anyone."

Henry Lee shook the rifle, and Ziggy stepped back. "What

the hell you mean 'show you where to find Angel?' She's in California with her mother."

Mel spoke clear and slow, "Henry Lee, drop the rifle and don't move. I have a gun directed at your head. I'm an excellent shot and have no qualms about blowing your head off."

The three men stepped forward and grabbed at the rifle as Henry Lee turned toward Mel. He appeared to be aiming at Mel, and she did the only thing her father and the Harbour Pointe SWAT team had taught her to do. She shot him.

He dropped to the ground, and the men rushed his writhing body and subdued him. Ziggy pulled rope from the tack and tied both Henry Lee's hands and legs to each other, hog-tie style.

Henry Lee continued to scream and holler, "Who the hell are you?"

Mel stood over him. "I'm your worst enemy. I'm Dee's best friend, and I'm not leaving this forest without finding Angel."

Mel called the sheriff, told them her location and that they had captured Henry Lee. Ziggy took a first-aid kit from his saddle bag and cleaned and bandaged the wound on Henry Lee's arm.

"Why'd you shoot me?" Henry Lee asked.

"I warned you to drop your weapon. Anyway, I'm a great shot. I wasn't going to kill you. Caught you in the fleshy part. No permanent damage."

"All this area is my property. You all were trespassing."

Ziggy asked, "Is that why you were holding a rifle on us?"

"Yeah. It's dark. I came out to hunt this morning. All I knew somebody was here. I didn't see you Ziggy. All I know this is Boudreaux property."

Frank added, "That's just plain bullshit. We're still in

Thicket country, nowhere near your place."

"Well, my blind is here."

"Well, that don't make it your land."

"All right boys, don't argue over the petty stuff. I'm here to bring Angel back home. Where is she, Henry Lee?"

"Honestly, I don't know what you're talking about. Damn that bullet burns."

"It's gonna hurt a lot worse if you don't tell us where she is," Ziggy said.

"I'm telling you, all of you, the last time I saw Angel, Dee walked out on me and took my Angel with her. I have no idea where my baby is."

Mel paced back and forth between her tent and Dizzy and tried to relive the kidnap timetable in her mind. Larry started to break camp, and they saddled the horses. Half an hour later, the sound of horses rapidly approaching shook the ground; and Mel stepped into the camp opening to greet Sheriff and several members of his posse.

Sheriff Marshall approached the clearing, "I heard some shots."

Ziggy answered, "One from Henry Lee flew wild. Mel shot him."

"Mel!"

"Is that so surprising?" she asked.

Sheriff shook his head and walked to the tree they had propped Henry Lee against. "You let a girl get the drop on you?"

"Shut the hell up." Henry Lee kicked dust at the sheriff's feet.

All the men laughed, and that only angered Henry Lee more. He struggled against the ropes to no avail.

"Let's call Red Opal. She'll have the news around the countryside before we get him back to jail."

"Don't you dare. Anything. I'll tell you anything you want to know."

With his serious face on, Sheriff leaned over, his elbow on his knee and said, "Henry Lee. It's this simple. We want Angel, and she better be alive for your sake, or you'll never get out of the Big Thicket alive today."

Chapter Thirty-Six

Henry Lee continued to maintain his ignorance on the 'Where's Angel?' issue throughout the entire ride to the third squad's location where they had bedded down the previous night. Their spot appeared to be an unpaved road between two large stands of pines.

"Why didn't we just drive in?" She asked when they pulled up and stopped.

Larry told her, "This is a fire road the forest department cut through here. They do this every so many miles through the forest. Good for easy entrance and exit if a fire were to start."

"What do we do now?" Mel asked.

The sheriff replied, "You and Henry Lee are leaving us here."

"Just me and him riding into the sunset?"

"No, actually..." the sound of copter blades approached the area.

Mel squinted up into the haze as the black copter hovered above and lowered a harness on a line. "Oh, I don't think so," she said. "I don't like to fly. Actually, I'm afraid to fly. I have bad dreams about crashing."

"Mel, we need your mount as an extra. So you can't ride back. I can't spare a man to take you two back through the forest. It doesn't look like we're going to catch the second guy that soon. I can't go in right now, and here's the good part. I've got a Ranger on board the copter who'll accompany you and Henry Lee to the police station."

"What's the good part?"

"You get to interrogate Henry without any of us there." Sheriff motioned to the circle of men, some of whom sat their mounts, while others stood around and drank coffee.

"Including the Ranger. He won't interfere, either?"

Sheriff crossed himself, "Cross my heart. He and copter will return here after they've dropped you and Henry Lee off."

"Oh, don't say 'dropped off,'" Mel whined.

"Don't be a pussy. You just captured Henry Lee. Be strong now," Sheriff kept talking dribble to distract Mel, as he helped her into the harness and gave a circular motion with his arm to the pilot to bring the cable up with Mel safely locked in the harness. Above the whirring of the blades, everyone on the ground could hear Mel say the longest version of, "S H I T!" they'd ever heard all of Mel's way to the safety of the aircraft.

Gina and Joanna stood outside the jail and waved as the copter landed and offloaded the frightened Mel, the bloody Henry Lee, and the cool-because-I-never-sweat Texas Ranger.

"Welcome the conquering hero," Gina said, as she applauded.

The Ranger locked Henry Lee behind bars in the same cell Mel spent a night in, gave Mel the key, shook her hand, tipped his white Stetson to all the ladies. Without another word, he re-boarded the copter and returned to the posse.

"Do they always look so cool? Starched white shirt, sharp

crease in those black pants, great hat, shiny badge, perfect teeth," Mel asked.

"Great butt," Gina added with a nod.

Joanna swatted Gina's butt with her apron, "Honestly. I can't believe you said that."

"Well, it's the truth."

They all chuckled.

"Anyway, ladies. We got no guys around to bug us. I feel like Dolly Parton in the movie, 'Nine to Five.' What we do have here all bound and trussed up is..."

In unison, they replied, "Henry Lee Boudreaux."

Mel opted for a warm shower and change of clothes at Joanna's house, followed by breakfast at Opals.

Joanna told Opal, "Henry Lee's gonna need some breakfast."

"How'd they catch him?"

"THEY didn't catch him," Gina said.

"I shot him," Mel volunteered and chuckled through her spoonful of gravy and grits.

Opal walked over to the booth, "Well then, your breakfast is on me this morning." She wiped her right hand on an apron and extended it to Mel, "I'd like to shake your hand."

"Thank you."

"Now if the bastard will just tell me where Angel is, it will have been worth all the effort," Mel said.

Mel's phone vibrated. She cleaned her mouth on a napkin and answered it. "Good morning. John Wayne here."

"Mel is that you? I have some good news," Johnnie said in his lilting voice.

"Me too. You first."

"Dee is sort of out of her coma. She's not responding, but her eyes track you when you're in the room. She can blink. X-Ray's getting clearance from her doctors to talk with her after lunch."

"That's great." Mel said to the others, "Dee's out of a coma."

A collective cheer filled the near-full café. Even truckers passing through who didn't even know her cheered.

"What's your news?" Johnnie asked.

"I shot Henry Lee this morning."

"Jesus Mel. You didn't have to go that far. What happened?"

"It's a long story. It's a flesh wound. Right now he's in jail, and I'm going to interview him after my breakfast."

"Where the hell have you been? I've been trying to reach you for two days?"

"Tracking two escaped convicts on horseback."

"No, seriously. Where were you?" Johnnie said.

Mel made mental notes as Henry Lee finished his lunch. She sat in the sheriff's chair a safe distance from Henry Lee's cell.

"Now that your belly is full, I think we have a lot to talk about."

"I want a lawyer."

"Fine. You can have an attorney. You have a right to one actually. When Sheriff gets back, he'll contact someone for you. But I'm nothing...a nobody, just a friend of Dee and Angel's who came to talk with Angel's daddy in jail today. We're just visiting here. I have no authority, no standing before the court, and nothing I can do will change the outcome planned for you." She stood as if to leave.

"What outcome you talking about?"

"Sheriff arresting you for attempted murder of Dee and possible murder of Angel."

Henry Lee jumped up, his metal food tray clattered to the

floor, "WHAT are you talking about woman?"

"Now that Dee's out of her coma..."

He grabbed the bars; his face shoved between them as he screamed, "What fucking coma?"

His outburst startled Mel, and she stepped farther away from him.

"Henry Lee, it's only a matter of hours, maybe minutes before Dee tells our California police department that it was you who grabbed and beat her almost to death. She's been in a coma for several days after your vicious attack. We thought she might die."

Henry Lee dropped to his bunk, his head in his hands, and sobbed like a baby.

"You're either a real fine actor, or you didn't play any part in hurting her."

He lay against the concrete block wall, sniffled, wiped his nose on his shirt sleeve, and shook his head. "I know people around here think I'm bad. I've had to, to survive. Oh, I may have knocked Dee around once or twice...when I was drunk, but almost kill her? Hurt my Angel? No way." He looked at Mel, "I love that woman. I love my baby." He wailed.

"Calm down. Do you want a drink of water or something?"

"I want outta here."

"I can't help you there. We have to wait for Sheriff Marshall. In the meantime, let's talk."

Mel returned to the chair and sat.

Henry Lee's body language changed, too, as he turned toward Mel and leaned sideways against the wall. "Shoot," he said.

"Did you follow Dee to San Diego and hurt her?"

"I never been to San Diego."

"Do you know who might have hurt Dee?"

He shook his head.

"Did you take Angel from her school?"

He shook his head. Resigned he responded, "Lady, I didn't even know Angel was missing, or that you was looking for me until this morning when you shot me. Slim and me been fishing. I don't know what you're talking about."

"Where's your high school graduation ring?"

"My what?" He looked at his hands. "Last time I saw that ring, it was on a chest of drawers in my parent's home."

"How long ago?"

"Years. Ten, maybe twenty. Since I work around saws and machinery, I took that thing off, oh, long time ago. You know, so that I wouldn't rip off a finger or my hand."

Mel nodded. "Did you know anything about a spleen being delivered here to the sheriff's office?"

Henry Lee's puzzled look became a stare. He turned toward space as if trying to catch the concept, then said, "Lady, I don't even know what a spleen is."

Chapter Thirty-Seven

Mel said, "A spleen is an organ that sits in the left upper part of your abdomen, tucked behind the lower margins of the rib cage. Right here." She stood and pointed out where her spleen would be found."

"Maybe Angel wasn't born with one," Henry Lee suggested.

"Yes, we're all born with one."

He thought for a minute, "Can we live without it?"

"Yes, of course, but our immune system is seriously compromised."

"What does that mean?"

"We're prone to infection, even death without one."

"Maybe she lost her spleen then, but is alive somewhere and doing fine," Henry Lee said.

"Maybe she's a Jane Doe in a hospital somewhere and can't tell anyone who she is."

Henry Lee stood. "I don't take to talk like that." He paced the length of the cell.

"You're right. Let's try to think positive," Mel calmed him down.

"If she's all right, why hasn't someone sent us a ransom note or contacted me, or Dee, or the police?"

"That's a damn good question. I don't know the answer."

Henry slammed his hands against the bars, "Hey, wait a minute. How do you know the spleen even belonged to Angel?"

"It's called DNA, Henry Lee," Mel said.

Mel educated him on the salient points of DNA. Even with his limited gene pool, Henry Lee strained to comprehend the procedure and nodded his head and asked questions throughout Mel's simply drawn diagrams and explanation.

She continued to interrogate Henry Lee for several hours. He endeavored to reconstruct his whereabouts during the time of Angel's kidnapping and Dee's assault often using the phases of the moon and his special fishing spots as sources of his recall.

He gave Mel names of people who might have a grudge against him and be framing him for the crimes and shared potential locations where Angel's body might be found. For those two things: the people with grudges and potential local grave sites, Mel needed a pencil and lots of paper. Henry Lee had been a real bad boy.

Throughout the long afternoon, his moods swung from calm to rage as he recounted specific individuals and clans around the countryside who didn't like him or his family. Mel kept the pencil moving and assured him that the sheriff would check out each and every lead. He vowed to do it himself and quickly if only she'd let him go free.

The sheriff's phone rang several times during the interview: one about some hogs that got loose on the Merkel property and another about a dead deer on the highway. Mel took down the locations and assured the callers that while she wasn't Sheriff Marshall's new secretary, she'd see he received the message when the escapee was caught.

Both asked, "Why'd you answer the phone then?"

To which she explained she was a visitor at Joanna and Gina's and just happened to be at the sheriff's office. Both callers wished her a nice vacation.

She made a few phone calls herself; including one to Lucas' cell phone where she left another message, one to X-Ray, and the last to Johnnie. As she shut her cell phone down, the sheriff's phone rang again.

"Damn, this place is busy," Henry Lee said.

"Sheriff's office, this is Mel speaking."

"Mom said I should call," Gina said.

"Hi. What about?"

"She wants to know how long you're going to be and if you'd like to have dinner with us tonight?"

"Not much longer now. I'd love dinner. How will I find your home?"

"I'll come get you. Would you plan on staying the night? Mom says with one convict still on the loose; she'd rather you not stay alone at the cabin. She says to tell you, 'There's safety in numbers, and we have some guns.'"

"I love guns, and that's a splendid idea. Give me thirty minutes."

Judge Marshall opened the door when she hung up the phone. "Good evening. I'm just closing the courthouse for the day, and Sheriff called and asked me to drop by and make sure you hadn't killed Henry Lee yet." He snickered.

"No, we're doing fine," Mel said, as she turned to Henry Lee. "We are, aren't we?"

Henry Lee rubbed his shaggy salt-and-pepper beard and

shrugged, "Yeah. I'd do much better if you let me outta here."

Mel said, "He thinks if we let him out he can do a faster and more efficient investigation than Sheriff can in finding Angel."

"Right." Judge Marshall rubbed his ample stomach and yawned. "You got something for me?"

Mel tossed the jail key ring to Judge. "I guess we need to feed Henry Lee."

"I'll drop by Opal's on my way home. Anything special you want?"

Henry Lee responded, "Ask her to send me extra cornbread and some buttermilk. Damn, I love that woman's cooking."

They heard footsteps approaching the landing and Judge opened the door to greet Bobby Gene. "Hey."

"Hi, guys. I heard Henry Lee was here and thought I'd stop by."

"I don't need you aggravating me," Henry Lee said.

"That's what brothers-in-law are for...for keeping you in line. Ain't that right?" Bobby Gene said smiling.

"I guess," Judge said.

"You heard about Dee?" Mel asked.

"I did. I am so happy. She's gonna be all right now, isn't she?"

"I don't believe she's out of the woods just yet. But she has regained consciousness, and our police department is talking with her. We hope to at least verify who did this to her. Henry Lee swears it wasn't him."

Henry Lee nodded, "That's for damn sure."

"You whipped on her before," Bobby Gene said.

Judge stepped between them, "Now you two, stop squabbling. You been doing that since you were babes. Grow up. Both of you."

They turned their backs to each other and grumbled.

"Lord, can you see Mel how much trouble these two have given me all these years?"

"They look like a handful."

"Believe me. If they had any bail money, I'd be a rich, rich man."

"I should check your bandage for infection before we go," Mel changed the subject since she hadn't paid her full bail yet either.

He stuck his arm between the bars, and Mel lifted the bandage. "Ah, a nice clean flesh wound, just like my daddy taught me."

"You didn't have to shoot me," he grumbled.

"I love that, you know? Everyone in town's heard that you been shot by a girl." Bobby Gene and Judge Marshall laughed, as Judge motioned for them to follow him out the door.

Chapter Thirty-Eight

Joanna and Gina lived in a small frame home surrounded by more of the Big Thicket. Their pebble-covered road led the way through a mile or so of large groves of pine and conifers to a similar opening as that of the cabin. Gina stopped the truck in the circular drive and Slick, the golden lab, bounced around the corner of the house and sat wagging his tail to greet them.

Colorful zinnias and an herb area filled with scented mint and rosemary hugged the freshly painted house on either side of a large wooden deck. Joanna wiped her hands on an apron and pushed the screen door open. "Welcome."

"Hi," Mel said. "What a darling home."

"We love it here."

Mel inhaled, "I can see and smell why."

Both Joanna and Gina chuckled at the comment.

"I heard you can see the air in LA. Is that right?" Gina asked.

"On many days you can. That's true."

"Ugh."

"Not healthy." Mel grabbed her backpack from the truck and stooped to pet Slick.

"Come on into our humble abode."

Chintz curtains fluttered in the breeze caused by the closing door. Although modest furnishings filled the living room, they matched in hues of blues and yellows to the kitchen and dining room beyond.

Beige linoleum with tiny yellow specks covered the floors. Rag shag rugs scattered in front of each seating area warmed the living area. Gina caught Mel looking at them, "I made those myself from old clothes that I shredded."

"You hooked those yourself?"

"Yeah. We learned about it in Home Ec classes."

"I think they're beautiful."

Gina beamed. "Let me show you your room."

Mel followed her down a short hallway to a pink bedroom where a Brittany and Justin poster hung on the closet door, and a rose-colored lava lamp sat on a nearby desk filled with school books. "I can't do this to you. This is your room."

"It's no problem. Really. Mom and me will bunk for a few days. Please."

From the kitchen, Joanna called out, "We wouldn't ask if we didn't want you here with us. Now drop your backpack and help me with dinner."

In a garden behind the house, they pulled fresh green onions, a tomato, a couple of summer squash, and Gina taught Mel how to dig for potatoes. Mel proudly boasted three and carried them to the sink to wash.

"Smell them," Gina said.

Mel said, "Like fresh dirt – that's what life is all about, Gina. Back to basics. I love the smell of vegetables without DDT and sprays, food without hormones."

"The country...it's all I know. You know, I've always dreamed of going to Hollywood and becoming a movie star. I'm a good actress. I love Shakespeare. Do you know any real movie stars?"

"I've done some work in the motion picture industry, you know as an investigator. It's my job to keep the star's names out of the news," she winked. "If you know what I mean?"

Gina set the table, Joanna chopped the vegetables, and Mel prepared the salad.

Joanna said, "I've always told Gina that her chances of being discovered are small. Although she is a fine actress and..."

"And I get all the starring roles in our local plays."

"I'm sure you do. You're a bright and very beautiful young lady," Mel said. "But your mother's right. There are millions of people around the world who dream like you do. Start small in your community and finish school. Get into a good college, hopefully, one with a strong drama department. These things don't happen overnight.

"In the meantime, stay away from drugs and alcohol, don't get pregnant, maintain those high values that your mother taught you, and your chances will be greatly enhanced."

Joanna, with her back to Gina, mouthed a "Thank you," to Mel. They both smiled.

Gina said, "Bummer."

After dinner, the trio took their coffee cups and sat on the deck. Gina and Slick played ball for a while as darkness set in over the tree-line.

Mel's cell rang, and she answered.

"Hi, Johnnie...of course, I knew it'd be you. Who else would call me at this hour? What's the news on Dee?"

Joanna and Gina could only hear Mel's side of the conversation, but clearly, the report wasn't favorable.

"She what?"

"You gotta be kidding me?"

"That bastard." She slammed the phone shut. "What's Opal's number? That lying bastard doesn't get any extra cornbread tonight."

Chapter Thirty-Nine

Mel tossed and turned all night. At one point unable to sleep any further, she slipped out of bed, pulled her jeans over her underwear, and sat on the deck barefooted patting Slick. Dew that glistened on every fern and leaf reflected the early morning light as dawn broke.

She heard stirring inside the house, then the smell of coffee brewing drew her back into its warmth. Gina dropped bread into the toaster, set out butter and jelly, and placed three coffee cups on the kitchen counter. "Breakfast?" she whispered.

"Bless your heart. I can wait on myself."

"No. This is what I do. It's my way of waiting on my mom sometimes."

"You're a good daughter."

"Sometimes I'm not."

"You're a teenage girl. You're doing the best you can with your hormones."

Gina giggled.

"You've been a good friend to me during my time here, and I want to thank you."

She blushed, "You're welcome. You know, you're the most successful woman I know."

"No, I'm not. Your mom is. After all, she supports you, loves you, and someday soon I hope, you'll have a new daddy."

"You think so?" Gina's butter knife stopped in mid-air.

"She's crazy about Sheriff Marshall, and it's easy to see that he's crazy about her."

Joanna shuffled into the kitchen, her pink slippers slid over the threshold in time to hear, "Who's crazy about her?" She yawned and stretched.

Gina giggled, "With your hair up in curlers and goo on your face like that, we sure ain't talking about you."

Mel and Gina laughed. Joanna yawned again and scratched her tiny belly through a tattered checked-colored bathrobe.

"Honestly, Mother. We have guests."

"Get over it, girl," Joanna grumbled, as she poured her coffee and sat at the kitchen table.

Gina shook her head; her eyes rolled up to the ceiling in disgust and embarrassment.

"Good morning you two," Mel said in her most cheerful voice. "I'm not a morning person either. Gina, the older you get, you won't be an early riser either, believe me."

"Listen to her," Joanna said.

"Can you tell us about Dee?" Gina asked.

"Yeah, well that's my biggest problem of the morning. Henry Lee lied to me. He said he didn't harm Dee in San Diego. Said he'd never been in San Diego. Said he and Slim had been fishing up on Caddo Lake. Dee told our cops that he grabbed her off the street, beat her senseless, then tossed her out of the car."

"Wow," Gina said.

"Yeah." Mel's phone rang. "Good morning. Hi, Lucas."

The girls cleaned up the kitchen and tried not listen to her one-sided conversation.

"That's great. I have some things to settle up here before leaving for home."

"A couple of days maximum."

"Can we take a boat instead?"

"I don't like to fly."

"We'll argue about that when I see you."

"Love ya too. Bye."

"Ooh, that sounds like a fella," Gina said.

"His name's Lucas. He's from Houston actually, but working in Liberia right now. He's going to join me for a brief vacation when I get home. I'm going to need it."

"Going anywhere special?"

"He's talking about Catalina?"

"And you have to fly there?" Gina asked.

"It's a quaint little island off the California coast. I'd rather go by boat."

Gina hugged her dish towel. "That's so romantic. Flying off to an island vacation." She hummed and danced a bit out of the room.

Joanna shook her head, "That girl. Her head's always in the clouds."

"She's very level-headed for a teenager. I've always believed drama is a major food for teenagers. I'm from California. Believe me, if you could meet some of those teenagers, you'd realize what a marvelous job you've done as a single parent."

"That's sweet of you for saying. Thank you."

"I'm off to beat the hell out of Henry Lee this morning. How can I reach Sheriff to bring him up to date?"

Joanna pulled a walkie-talkie from the front seat of her truck, clicked it on to a sputter of exchanges between several voices and said, "Wait until they quit jabbering, then press this button down and hold it while you talk. Then release and wait for a response. Tell Sheriff I said 'good morning.' I gotta get dressed. Excuse me."

She lifted her tattered bathrobe so it wouldn't drag the ground and disappeared into the house, as she pulled the pink curlers from her hair.

God, how she loves that man, Mel thought.

"One thing's for sure," she heard Sheriff say to someone else, "He's not in our grid. We're packing in until we hear further from you. Over."

"Roger and out," came the reply.

With no other message Mel pressed the button, "Sheriff, this is Mel." There was a long pause.

"Howdy. Over."

"Joanna says to tell you 'good morning.'" She paused, then added, "Over."

"Back at her. We're coming in. Over."

"I heard. We have news, and it isn't good. Over."

"Yeah? Over."

"Henry Lee lied to me. Dee told our police that he put her there in the hospital. Over."

"Where are you? Over."

"At Joanna's home now and heading to the jail to beat the hell outta him. Over."

"Not if I don't beat you to the punch. Over."

During Mel's ride into town, the black helicopter flew over the tree tops toward the jail; and minutes later she heard its engine roar into the air once again.

Gina pulled up to the courthouse. The small parking lot was so cramped with trucks she let Mel out on the graveled shoulder a short distance from the building. Mel waved, walked into the lobby, and took the stairs to the jail above. Before she reached the turn in the stairway landing, she heard loud, angry voices. She opened the door in time to see some Texas justice.

Sheriff and two of his deputies and took Henry Lee's breakfast tray away, and seriously questioned him as only the "good ole boys" can. Mel turned on her heels and left. They didn't need any help from a city slicker.

Chapter Forty

As she stopped the Jimmy in the dirt road near the cabin, a black truck blocked her path to the lean-to. She honked and jumped out with her backpack. Bobby Gene appeared in the open doorway.

"Howdy." He waved.

"Whatcha doing?" she asked.

"Joanna said I could stop by and pick up some bass lures," Bobby Gene smiled and held up two lures; one in each hand. "I hope you don't mind."

"No. It's her cabin. I need to gather my things together."

"Leaving us so soon?"

"I think I'll go into Beaumont tonight and stay in a hotel," a decision she made as she spoke, "Then catch a plane home tomorrow."

"What about Angel? Are we ever gonna find her?"

"I hope so. I just left the jail, and Sheriff Marshall has his arms around everything."

"Dee's my baby sister. You know that I'll kill Henry Lee if he did this?"

"I suspect you will if someone doesn't beat you to it."

"I suppose you're looking forward to getting home."

"You're so right."

"Where do you live?" Bobby Gene asked.

"In Harbour Pointe."

"Is that anywhere near Seal Beach and Long Beach?"

"Pretty close. Ever been to California?"

"Naw. I seen pictures of the beach and all and things in movies, but I never been there." Bobby Gene stepped out of the doorway toward his truck. "I'll be saying goodbye for now."

"You got all you need?" Mel asked.

"Yep. Going fishing."

"Is that all you guys do on your days off?"

"What else is there? This ain't hunting season."

"When did that ever stop Texans?"

Bobby Gene laughed as he drove off.

The cabin appeared messier than Mel's last visit, and she straightened everything as best she could and swept away cobwebs and some mouse leavings. She packed and caught a ride to Beaumont with one of Joanna's neighbors who was going grocery shopping in Vidor. The friend dropped Mel off at a hotel near the airport. After a bath, Mel called home.

"Hi, Johnnie, what's happening?"

"Dee's getting stronger and stronger. The nurses got her out of bed this afternoon, and she walked a bit."

"That's really great news."

"She's still groggy, and the jury is still out on her brain damage, but she has a strong will."

"She's gonna need it. I have a sinking feeling that we're never going to find Angel."

"It sickens me to think that. I saw the prison break story on television. They caught one. Did you catch the other?"

"No. I left the hunt. But I did catch Henry Lee."

"Caught and shot, huh?"

"Yep, just a flesh wound."

"Good girl. Where'd you get the gun?"

"I'm a deputy. Can you believe they actually empowered me to carry one?"

"You are so funny," Johnnie said. "They sure don't know you very well. What's next?"

"I want to talk with Dee. Did her friend Greg from AA have anything new for us?"

"Nothing. I hit a dead end there."

"How'd Dee arrive at the hospital? Did you question the ambulance drivers?"

"Didn't come by EMT. Nurses told X-Ray they found Dee all alone, laying on a gurney just outside the double doors."

"Interesting. It's a long drive from San Diego where she disappeared to Harbour View. She sure didn't walk in."

"I agree, that's curious."

"I gotta go. I need some sleep on a real bed in my air conditioned room, with no snakes, no alligators, and no escaped convicts."

"Hugs. See you tomorrow."

Mel slept fretfully. Angel's face haunted her. Mel cried out several times and woke herself up drenched in sweat.

Does this mean I can't leave town without you sweet baby? Mel said out loud, as she lay back on her pillow and shed a few tears for a little-lost child. She gritted her teeth and vowed to find Angel no matter what. Going to California tomorrow didn't mean she wouldn't be back if she had to. She would bring Angel home.

Johnnie picked Mel up at John Wayne Airport, and they drove straight to Harbour View. "Rosa packed you some food," he said. "She knows what airline food can be."

"That woman is something. But all I did in Texas was eat. Lots of carbs, cornbread, red beans, and rice. Good stuff. I even learned to love grits and gravy for breakfast."

"What's grits?"

"To die for."

Mel dug through the bag and found a homemade tamale, which she inhaled. She set the apple aside for later.

Johnnie and Mel entered Dee's hospital room to find her watching TV. Dee smiled in recognition. *That's a good sign*, Mel thought.

"So, how's our favorite client today?"

Dee nodded and continued to grin.

Mel patted her arm. "I just flew in from Zavalla. Do you feel strong enough to answer just a few questions?"

Dee nodded.

"We found Henry Lee."

Dee's smile faded.

"He says he didn't hurt you this time."

Dee turned her face away from the twosome.

"Look at me, Dee. I know you can't talk just yet, so let's use the one and two blink concept. One blink for 'No' and two blinks for 'Yes.' Can you do that for me?"

Dee sighed, turned back to Mel and Johnnie and blinked twice.

In San Diego, and he left to go to the bathroom. Right?"

Two blinks.

"Did you go outside on your own?"

Two blinks.

"So, Henry Lee didn't come in there and take you out?"

One blink.

"Was he in a truck or alone or with someone?"

Dee's panic expression stopped them.

Johnnie said, "Mel, that's a compound question. Dee was he in a truck?"

No blinks.

Mel resumed questioning. "Was he alone?"

Two blinks.

"Did he drag you into a truck?"

No blinks.

"A car?"

No blinks. Her eyes darted the room as if trying to escape.

Confused, Mel leaned over very close to Dee's face, "Now listen to me carefully. I've interrogated Henry Lee, and so has Sheriff Marshall. He swears he's never been to San Diego; doesn't even know where the city is located. He loves you very much. He may not be able to show it in positive ways like a normal person would. But beating you from time to time when he's drunk is his way of expressing himself. It doesn't mean he doesn't love you and Angel very much.

"Don't frame him if you're mad at him. Don't frame him if you're angry because Angel is missing. Don't do it to get back at all the bad things he's done to you. He may be the key to finding Angel yet. What I'm thinking is you may be mistaken about him beating you up in San Diego. If I'm correct, now would be a good time to tell me."

Dee grabbed Mel's hand, her eyes pled forgiveness. Then she wailed through the tubes in her throat like a trapped animal.

Chapter Forty-One

Mel wrote a retraction of Dee's former statement and had Dee sign it. Dee's hand quivered while she wrote her name.

"Nothing's going to happen to you for lying."

Johnnie added, "But you should have told the police the truth."

"I could have killed Henry Lee you know. I almost did."

Dee jerked her head; her wild eyes darkened at Mel's comment.

"Oh, it was just a little flesh wound. He had a rifle on two deputies, and I got a drop on him."

Dee relaxed, then smiled.

"See? You think that's funny, too. A girl getting a drop on old Henry Lee." Mel chuckled.

Two blinks in rapid succession followed, and Dee smiled through her tears.

"Do you know who did attack you?" Mel asked.

One blink.

Johnnie asked, "So, this was a random attack...from a perfect stranger?"

One blink. Dee put her hand up to touch the trach tube and coughed.

"Do you know how you got here to the hospital?"

One blink.

"Were you unconscious the entire trip from San Diego?"

Two blinks.

Mel turned to Johnnie, "Is it possible that you and Dee were followed to San Diego?"

"By whom?" Johnnie asked.

"I'm thinking Greg. He works here. I think he has a crush on Dee. I think he was concerned. You know how co-dependent AA folks are? Always trying to save others. He didn't know who you were; and after she was attacked, rather than get the bad guy, he opted to get Dee to safety."

"Why didn't he stop the attack if he cares so much?"

"Maybe he'd taken his eyes off the office for a few minutes. Went to potty, get a drink, something and when he returned, he found Dee, put her in his car and brought her to the hospital where he worked; where he knew she'd be well taken care of."

Dee, who had taken all this conversation in, grabbed Mel's hand and calmly blinked twice.

X-Ray walked into Dee's room. "Jesus. You been back two hours and already stirring up things."

Mel hugged him, "I love you too. Did you miss me?"

"Yes. No. Whatever." He shook her hug off in a loving way. "I heard you shot someone in Texas."

"I'm an official deputy. They even gave me a gun."

"That's no license to kill Jane Bond."

"It is if it's Henry Lee."

"Sheriff Marshall told me."

"Here's Dee statement. She's real sorry," Johnnie said.

Dee blinked twice to make sure everyone in the room saw her response.

"Listen, Dee; I'm going to take Greg to the station for questioning."

Fear rose in Dee's eyes again; she blinked once shutting her eyes hard for emphasis.

"It's not to arrest him. We just need to question him and see if he'd recognize your attacker."

Dee relaxed.

A uniformed nurse entered the room with a medicine tray. "I think Dee's had enough excitement. It's time for her medication and rest."

Mel picked up her purse; and as she patted Dee's arm, said, "We're going to leave you for tonight. Please rest..."

At that moment a panic-stricken Dee clutched her heart with a free hand, gasped for breath, and passed out. The heart monitor above her head ran a flat-line. The nurse pushed the emergency button on the wall and yelled, "Stat. Code Blue," then jumped astride Dee's body and began CPR.

Chapter Forty-Two

They trio paced the waiting room floor well into the night. The nurse and doctors worked miracles until Dee's heart stabilized, then rushed her into emergency surgery. By early morning, Dee remained in surgery, and more specialists had been called in to handle what one nurse told the trio were "unforeseen complications," which weren't fully explained.

X-Ray slept on a small vinyl love seat using some magazines as a pillow. Johnnie dozed on the floor with blankets that the hospital had provided. Mel had a lounge chair with foot stool but awoke with a pounding headache from her head leaning at an angle for hours. The smell of fresh-brewed coffee aroused them about the same time.

"Oh, I could use that," Mel said, as she rubbed her sore neck.

"Me too. Where're the donuts?" Johnnie asked.

A nurse assured him they'd be delivered soon.

X-Ray left to wash his face and upon returning yawned and said, "She's still in surgery. How much can a body take I wonder?"

"At least she's still alive. Should we call her family in Texas? Sheriff should probably be notified."

"The nurse talked with me last night and told me that her survival outlook appeared dim, so I called him. He'll notify the rest of the family."

"They must be frightened to death..." Mel said and was interrupted with some visitors who rushed into the waiting room.

"We were frightened plum to death. I never flew in such a small plane before," Sheriff said, as he led the small group that included Joanna and Gina into the room.

"It's so exciting," Gina said smiling. "I'm in Hollywood. I'm really in Hollywood."

Mel hugged Gina and Joanna and replied, "Not exactly, and certainly not for that reason."

"I know. I'm sorry she's hurting so much. But I'm so excited."

Sheriff asked, "How is Dee?"

"We're waiting for a report now. We get one about every hour," Johnnie said.

"Where's Henry Lee?" Mel asked.

"I left his sorry ass in jail for now until this is all sorted out."

They paced the small room, drank coffee, and ate donuts for the next twenty minutes until a man in surgical greens entered the room and pulled his mask to the top of his capped head.

"Good morning. I assume part of you are family."

Sheriff stepped forward. "I'm Sheriff Paul Ames Marshall. Dee's my sister. This is the Widow Thompson and her daughter Gina Gribow Thompson.

The doctor nodded to everyone after shaking Sheriff Marshall's hand. "I'm glad you're here. We need all the prayers we can get. Mrs. Boudreaux threw a blood clot that hit her heart. She had a complete cardiac arrest. Then pressure began to rise, causing swelling in her brain. We had to release that pressure all the while trying to prevent her from throwing other clots."

"Oh my Lord," Sheriff said, as he sat on the sofa dejected.

The doctor continued, "Mrs. Boudreaux's heart stopped several times during the operation. We had to place her on heart bypass to work on the brain problem."

"And now?" Johnnie asked.

"She's in Cardiac Care Unit in very critical condition. We'll know more in twelve to twenty-four hours."

"What are her chances of survival?"

"Ten, maybe twenty percent. Not much more than that right now. We need the swelling in the brain to go down. I'm sorry I can't be more optimistic.

"The good news is, she does have youth on her side. She's been quite a little fighter. She hung in with us all night."

"She is a fighter." Sheriff turned and walked out of the room. Mel motioned for Joanna to follow him.

Sheriff notified all the family on both sides who had telephones: the Boudreaux's and the Marshall's. He designated Tiny Opal's diner as the clearing house for all information to and from family members and interested parties. By noon, everyone was exhausted. Mel invited everyone to go home with her, rest, eat, and clean up. "There's nothing more we can do but worry, and we can do that at home," she told them. "I live very close, and we can get back here quickly."

Rosa had made up beds, put out fresh towels, and tossed

some quick salads and sandwiches by the time the group drove into the driveway. She smiled as she opened the door to greet everyone.

Gina said, "Wow," upon entering. She ran to the patio door, opened it, and rushed out to the edge of the deck toward the crashing ocean below the cliff. "Oh my God. I have died and gone to heaven."

Joanna looked around and meekly replied, "You must think we're real hicks."

Mel hugged her. "Come in here. I think no such thing. I married and divorced a very successful, yet asshole attorney." She added quickly, "And then my father died and left me a lot of money."

Joanna nodded.

Rosa introduced herself and ushered everyone to the patio table. She served iced tea and lemonade, inquired about Dee's condition, and left Mel with her guests.

"You even have a maid," Gina gushed.

"Not really. Rosa is part of my family, and she helps me out sometimes."

"And you drive a Mercedes," Gina whispered elaborately.

Mel whispered back, "And it's over twenty-years-old and on its last leg, mechanically speaking."

Johnnie spoke up, "That old orange-colored Mustang at the curb is mine. I call her the Pumpkin. She's a '56 model...a real classic."

"I love it," Gina said.

"Sit down and be quiet. Maybe I should have left you at home," Joanna said in a scolding way. "You're being such a pest."

"No. It's all right, really. She's just a teenager excited about coming to California."

"Did you find Bobby Gene to tell him about Dee?" Mel asked.

"Yeah, but he had to work," Sheriff said.

Mel turned. "I thought he went bass fishing."

"He doesn't bass fish. Whatever gave you that idea?"

"When I drove up to Joanna's cabin yesterday he was just coming out and holding two bass lures."

Joanna leaned in, "What?"

"He said you told him to drop by there for them."

Joanna said, "Well, he lied. I told him no such thing."

Chapter Forty-Three

X-Ray's cell phone rang. He answered it and walked away from the group on the patio to talk, then returned a few seconds later. "We have some news."

"Shoot," Mel said.

"That was Detective Rhonda Wilder from the San Diego Police Department."

"The one who took me to the coroner's office?" Mel asked.

"Yeah, her. Anyway, their department responded to a call about a mugger that some citizens chased down and caught. They questioned him, and he confessed to several attacks, including one on a woman who had stepped out of a doctor's office a few days ago. Seems she resisted him, and he beat the hell out of her, then fled."

"Damn," Mel said.

"Dee fits the woman's description."

"Damn," Sheriff Marshall said.

"If Greg followed Dee and Johnnie to San Diego, why didn't Greg save her?"

"That's a good question. I'll ask him," X-Ray said. "My

officers picked him up after work and right now he's going through mug books at the station."

Mel and Sheriff decided to return to the hospital and see if they could at least see Dee before they retired for the evening. Johnnie stayed behind and entertained Joanna and Gina with stories of movie stars and rock singers.

A CCU Nurse recognized Mel as a frequent visitor and whispered that they could visit Dee, but for just a few moments. "She remains in a deep coma," the nurse explained.

They approached her bed station and pulled the curtain aside. Dee's head was completely wrapped in white bandages. Tubes connected to pumps united her with the living. The rhythmic sounds of her pumping heart and bags of IV drips hung on either side of the bed. Her black-and-blue face appeared grotesquely abnormal; her eyes were swollen shut and matted with tears.

Sheriff inhaled and approached the bed. He squeezed her hands in love and kissed her bandaged forehead.

He and Mel stood there a few minutes in silence, then quietly withdrew. On the drive home, Mel spoke first, "You guys are a tight family."

"Is that a question?" Sheriff asked.

"More of a statement really."

"I guess we are in our own way. Not much prone to emotion. But we hang together when the going gets tough."

"I understand."

"I'm worried that we'll never find Angel."

"So am I."

"If you hadn't received that DNA report yourself, I wouldn't have believed it to match her spleen," Mel proffered.

"Well, I didn't exactly get either of the DNA reports direct from the lab."

"What does that mean?" Mel turned in her seat.

"Bobby Gene got both reports: the one on the spleen and mine, on his fax machine at the hospital. Remember, my fax machine is broken. He brought the test results over to my office."

"How do he and Henry Lee get along?"

"They're like oil and water, those two. Fought like Indians since they were kids. Bobby Gene never wanted Dee to marry Henry Lee."

"When we get home can you call the Texas lab and leave a message for them?"

"And tell them what?"

"It's more of an 'ask.' Ask them to fax a copy of both reports to my fax machine at home first thing tomorrow morning."

"What are you thinking?"

"I hope I'm wrong."

Mel set her alarm for six the following morning, but she heard her fax machine toss out paper before the alarm rang. She threw on a robe and dashed downstairs where she met Sheriff standing over it putting the papers in number order.

"Well?" She asked.

Sheriff sorted them, read through them several times, and stared dumbfounded into space. "It's hard to really interpret these tests from a medical sense, but what I make of it – there's no chance in hell that the spleen belonged to Angel nor did my DNA match the sample taken. I'll bet Bobby Gene changed the zero into a one-hundred. I can check it when I get home. Clearly, this report says 'zero.'" Then he bellowed raising everyone in the house, "That bastard. Why'd he do that for?"

"Lie to us?" Mel asked.

"Yes, damn it."

"He wanted to frame Henry Lee. Remember, his finger-prints were the only other ones on the box except our two, and I'm thinking it's more than a coincidence that he also delivered your mail." She paused. "Another thing, if he and Henry Lee had been childhood friends, he'd certainly have access to the Boudreaux home where Henry Lee told me his high school ring lay in plain sight on top of a chest of drawers. He told me he didn't wear the ring because of him working around so much machinery."

Sheriff pushed Mel aside, "Can I use your telephone? I'm gonna have that bastard arrested."

She grabbed his arm as he picked up the receiver and wrestled with him over it. Joanna and Gina met at the door of the office about the same time. Mel said, "You can't do that?"

"And you think you're going to stop me? I'm the fucking Sheriff." He pushed her away.

"Sheriff, Bobby Gene worked for a hospital and the morgue. I'm thinking he took a spleen from someone after surgery. He faked the DNA, so let's believe that Angel is alive; and so is the person who donated their spleen to Bobby Gene's scheme."

Joanna stepped in between them holding her robe close around her small frame. "Sheriff. Mel is right. If Bobby Gene lied about the test results, and God forgive me if I'm wrong, maybe he took Angel to frame Henry Lee too."

Sheriff sank in Mel's chair. "What are you talking about?"

"What if he knows where she is? If you have him arrested, he may never tell us. He may have harmed her, and we'll never find her. I'm beginning to think that it was really him who shot at me the first day I stayed in the cabin."

Gina cried, and Joanna hugged her for support. "Please

Paul Ames. Think this out. That's what you do best. Don't go in like the Texas Rangers," Joanna said.

Mel thought for a minute, then spoke, "We know that Angel would never have gone willingly with someone she didn't know. Dee assured me Angel knew the family rule on strangers."

"If Bobby Gene came after me at school, I'd go with him," Gina said.

Mel added, "I think Bobby Gene lied to me about being in California. He knew about Seal Beach and Long Beach and their proximity to where Dee lived. I think he took Angel."

Sheriff slammed his fist on the desk. "Damn it. If he's hurt her...."

"No," Mel interrupted that thought process. "Let's think this out. He wouldn't kill her. Our plan should include this scenario.

"Let's assume for a minute that Bobby Gene DID pick up Angel after school. Where could he take her and leave her that she wouldn't be suspicious of being left there for a long time without seeing her mother?"

Everyone paced the floor, then moved quietly out into the hall, through the living room and onto the patio. Mel prepared coffee and Gina joined her. "I let mom and Sheriff alone to think." She winked.

"Good idea. The ocean will clear their heads on a lot of unresolved issues," Mel smiled.

Mel carried a tray filled with two coffee cups, sugar, and cream. Through the slider they saw both Joanna and Paul Ames standing at the deck's edge, holding hands. Gina opened the door; and Mel slid the tray onto the table, then closed it behind her. She and Gina returned to the breakfast room and sat enjoying theirs.

"Gina, what are you thinking?" Mel asked.

"I think I'm going to get a new daddy."

Throughout the morning, Sheriff made a few well-placed phone calls to Texas family members using the deception of reporting Dee's current medical condition. Everyone asked about Angel. There wasn't a hint of impropriety in anyone's voice. Mel contacted X-Ray and Johnnie, who joined them for support and ideas.

Johnnie bought his favorite things from the office: butcher paper, black markers, and some tacks, which he used to mount the paper on one living room wall with Mel's blessing. He made one list of everyone Sheriff called. He made a list of everyone they could think of who didn't have a phone or any means of communicating with the outside world and that included computers, cells, fax machines, or nearby stores or homes with such items.

Sheriff said, "We've already been to Henry Lee's family's home, and I don't believe they would keep her from us."

Mel said, "They wouldn't help one bad son frame another bad son, would they?"

"Naw," was the collective response. "Not at Angel's expense."

Johnnie said, "We all agree, they love Angel. We'll mark them off the list."

Mel returned to the room. "Just talked with the hospital. There's no change."

"Is that good news?" Gina asked.

"We hope so," Mel replied.

Rosa arrived and began to make lunch. The doorbell rang, and Rosa answered it. "It's Mr. Lucas," she said and returned to the kitchen.

Mel rushed to greet him and kissed him long and hard.

Lucas rubbed her almost bald head, "What happened here?"

Mel replied, "It's a long story."

Gina swooned, "Oh my God. Is this your fella?"

Mel smiled and introduced Lucas as her "Texan" and Sheriff extended a hardy handshake, then sank into the sofa and re-focused on the butcher paper.

"What's going on here?" Lucas asked.

"We're trying to solve a crime," Gina said all smiles and flirting through every spoken word.

Gina's mother hit her shoulder and rolled her eyes. "Please," she pleaded. "Do not embarrass yourself or me."

"I'm not," she whispered, as she curled up on the sofa and played with her painted toenails.

Rosa sat lunch on the dining room table along with paper plates, napkins, and cold drinks. "You need brain power. Lunch is ready." She returned to the kitchen to work on completing a dinner that could be warmed later.

"What about...?" Joanna said several times during lunch.

So did Sheriff.

Then Gina asked nonchalantly, "When you guys were tracking the convicts did anyone go by the Alabama-Coushatta reservation?"

Sheriff responded, "That area was included in my search grid, but I didn't go by there. Why do you ask?"

"I think Boudreaux's got some family there. I remember one little Indian girl who came to school a few times. Claimed she and Angel were cousins."

"Why'd she quit coming to school?"

"I heard their horse went lame."

"What was her name? Do you remember?" Johnnie asked.

"It was something like Polly Anna. That's not exactly right, but it's close."

Sheriff picked up the kitchen phone and called the deputy at his office in Zavalla. "Did we cover the Indian reservation?"

"It was on our grid," he hollered. "Is there any team still out there?" Pause.

"Well, get them on the walkie-talkie and call me back at this number."

Minutes passed when the phone rang again. Sheriff answered.

"Yeah, tell the men to check every tepee, every hut, every chicken coop, every barn on that reservation. Tell them we're looking for Angel, and they can't leave the Big Thicket without her – alive and well. Call me back."

Chapter Forty-Four

The hours passed slowly. Sheriff and Joanna spent some time walking on the beach with Mel's hands-free phone. Rosa and Johnnie took Gina down the beach in the other direction toward the arcade and ice cream parlor at the game shop. Mel and Lucas sat on the deck and stared at the setting sun just above the horizon.

Their silence was broken by screams from below. Mel and Lucas rushed to the stairs that led from the cliff to the ocean floor to see Paul Ames and Joanna, shoes in hand, falling all over themselves and hugging and laughing.

"Well?" Mel hollered to them.

"They found her."

Joanna and Paul Ames reached the lower riser and ran up the steps. "They found her."

"Yeah, we hear you. She's all right?"

"She's fine." Joanna hugged Mel, and they swung around in a circle.

Lucas shook Sheriff's hand.

There wasn't a dry eye in the sand that evening.

Sheriff spoke, "Our unit found Angel just sitting there playing corn stalk dolls with her 'cousin,' if you can call her that, inside a teepee. Angel thought she was on school break – a vacation of sorts. Bobby Gene picked Angel up after school and told her that Dee would join her in a few weeks."

"Didn't her caregivers get anxious when Dee didn't at least call and check up on Angel?" Mel asked.

"The Alabama-Coushatta's aren't like California Indians, Mel. They may be a sovereign nation, but they don't have a casino. They don't even have a phone. They mind their own business and don't ask questions," Sheriff explained.

Joanna added, "And Gina remembered their only horse went lame." She hugged Gina as did the entire group.

Sheriff ordered his deputies to pick up Bobby Gene and hold him for extradition to California on kidnapping and child endangerment charges. He also told them, "Throw his sorry ass in the same cell with Henry Lee, and make sure Henry Lee gets the whole truth and nothing but the truth. Then lock the jail and go home. You heard me." He hung up the phone. "I'll teach that bastard."

Gina asked, "If the spleen wasn't Angel's, then whose was it?"

Sheriff answered her, "Honey, we may never know. Bobby Gene worked at the hospital, and I can see now how he might have taken one, say after an operation when it was removed. They're supposed to properly dispose of excised body parts, but this is Bobby Gene we're talking about."

Mel said, "One sick bastard."

Everyone nodded.

X-Ray asked, "Don't you know a judge who can prepare those papers and get them moved through the system quickly?"

"Assuming Bobby Gene survives the night, you bet I do."
The sheriff replied and made his next call.

Judge Marshall answered on the second ring. After hearing
the story, he told his brother, "Hell yes. I'll hire another plane
and take Angel into Beaumont to have her checked out medically first; then we'll fly Angel into John Wayne Airport. Look
for us tomorrow afternoon latest. Hell yes. I'll call ya."

"Speaking of flying," Lucas said. "How about a lovely rest-
ful weekend in Catalina?"

"There are a lot of loose ends here," Mel said. "For one
thing, I owe the city of Zavalla more than six-hundred dollars
in fines. So I gotta work. Dee's still in a coma..."

Sheriff Paul Ames Marshall said, "Consider that fine, an
engagement present to you from the grateful citizens of Zavalla."

Joanna added, "Don't worry about us. We can handle it
from now on. You two love birds take some time off. I've got
Johnnie and Rosa to help me."

"Could you all stay here for the weekend at least?"

"We wouldn't miss it for the world. Maybe we could go to
Disneyland," Gina said.

"Sure. Johnnie's got an annual pass he'd love to share with
you," Mel said. "Are you sure?"

Everyone gave her a resounding vote of confidence.

She mumbled, "You know I hate flying. How about the
float boat?"

Lucas whispered in her ear, "We can get to that hotel room
a lot faster in a plane," then he kissed her on the ear.

"Sold cowboy."

Mel packed a few things and tossed the car and house keys
to Joanna, and with hugs all around she and Lucas escaped like
elopers in the night.

After dinner, Johnnie and Gina sat at the dining room table and plotted their trip to Disneyland. Joanna and Paul Ames snuggled on the couch and watched television. Toward the end of Sheriff's favorite show, "Cops," the newscaster interrupted with an important news flash.

"The Coast Guard is searching the waters off Catalina tonight for a plane reported missing with a pilot and two passengers aboard...."

www.ingramcontent.com/pod-product-compliance
Lightning Source LLC
Chambersburg PA
CBHW031409250626
47155CB00004B/1471